NOT JUST THE BOSS'S PLAYTHING

BY

CAITLIN CREWS

MILLS & BOON

First published in Great Britain 2013
by Mills & Boon, an imprint of Harlequin (UK) Limited,
Large Print edition 2014
Eton House, 18-24 Paradise Road,
Richmond, Surrey, TW9 1SR

© 2013 Caitlin Crews

ISBN: 978 0 263 24038 2

Harlequin (UK) Limited's policy is to use papers that are natural, renewable and recyclable products and made from wood grown in sustainable forests. The logging and manufacturing processes conform to the legal environmental regulations of the country of origin.

Printed and bound in Great Britain
by CPI Antony Rowe, Chippenham, Wiltshire

NOT JUST
THE BOSS'S
PLAYTHING

CHAPTER ONE

TORTURE WOULD BE preferable to this.

Nikolai Korovin moved through the crowd ruthlessly, with a deep distaste for his surroundings he made no effort to hide. The club was one of London's sleekest and hottest, according to his assistants, and was therefore teeming with the famous, the trendy and the stylish.

All of whom appeared to have turned up tonight. In their slick, hectic glory, such as it was. It meant Veronika, with all her aspirations to grandeur, couldn't be far behind.

"Fancy a drink?" a blank-eyed creature with masses of shiny black hair and plumped-up lips lisped at him, slumping against him in a manner he imagined was designed to entice him. It failed. "Or anything else? Anything at all?"

Nikolai waited impatiently for her to stop that insipid giggling, to look away from his chest and find her way to his face—and when she did, as expected, she paled. As if she'd grabbed hold of the devil himself.

She had.

He didn't have to say a word. She dropped her hold on him immediately, and he forgot her the moment she slunk from his sight.

After a circuit or two around the loud and heaving club, his eyes moving from one person to the next as they propped up the shiny bar or clustered around the leather seating areas, cataloging each and dismissing them, Nikolai stood with his back to one of the giant speakers and simply waited. The music, if it could be called that, blasted out a bass line he could feel reverberate low in his spine as if he was under sustained attack by a series of concussion grenades. He almost wished he was.

He muttered something baleful in his native Russian, but it was swept away in the deep, hard thump and roll of that terrible bass. *Torture.*

Nikolai hated this place, and all the places like it he'd visited since he'd started this tiresome little quest of his. He hated the spectacle. He hated the waste. Veronika, of course, would love it—that she'd be *seen* in such a place, in such company.

Veronika. His ex-wife's name slithered in his

head like the snake she'd always been, reminding him why he was subjecting himself to this.

Nikolai wanted the truth, finally. She was the one loose end he had left, and he wanted nothing more than to cut it off, once and for all. Then she could fall from the face of the planet for all he cared.

"I never loved you," Veronika had said, a long cigarette in her hand, her lips painted red like blood and all of her bags already packed. "I've never been faithful to you except by accident." Then she'd smiled, to remind him that she'd always been the same as him, one way or another: a weapon hidden in plain sight. "Needless to say, Stefan isn't yours. What sane woman would have *your* child?"

Nikolai had eventually sobered up and understood that whatever pain he'd felt had come from the surprise of Veronika's departure, not the content of her farewell speech. Because he knew who he was. He knew *what* he was.

And he knew her.

These days, his avaricious ex-wife's tastes ran to lavish Eurotrash parties wherever they were thrown, from Berlin to Mauritius, and the well-manicured, smooth-handed rich men who attended such events in droves—but Nikolai knew she was in London now. His time in the Russian Special Forces had taught him many things, much of which remained etched deep into that cold, hard stone where his heart had never been, and finding a woman with high ambitions and very low standards like Veronika? Child's play.

It had taken very little effort to discover that she was shacking up with her usual type in what amounted to a fortress in Mayfair: some dissipated son of a too-wealthy sheikh with an extensive and deeply bored security force, the dismantling of which would no doubt be as easy for Nikolai as it was entertaining—but would also, regrettably, cause an international incident.

Because Nikolai wasn't a soldier any longer. He was no longer the Spetsnaz operative who could do whatever it took to achieve his goals—with a deadly accuracy that had won him a healthy respect that bordered on fear from peers and enemies alike. He'd shed those skins, if not what lay beneath them like sinew fused to steel, seven years ago now.

And yet because his life was nothing but an exercise in irony, he'd since become a philanthropist, an internationally renowned wolf in the ill-fitting clothes of a very soft, very fluffy sheep. He ran the Korovin Foundation, the charity he and his brother, Ivan, had begun after Ivan's retirement from Hollywood action films. Nikolai tended to Ivan's fortune and had amassed one of his own thanks to his innate facility with investment strategies. And he was lauded far and near as a man of great compassion and caring, despite the obvious ruthlessness he did nothing to hide.

People believed what they wanted to believe. Nikolai knew that better than most.

He'd grown up hard in post-Soviet Russia, where brutal oligarchs were thick on the ground and warlords fought over territory like starving dogs—making him particularly good at targeting excessively wealthy men and the corporations they loved more than their own families, then talking them out of their money. He knew them. He understood them. They called it a kind of magic, his ability to wrest huge donations from the most reluctant and wealthiest of donors, but Nikolai saw it as simply one more form of warfare.

And he had always been so very good at war. It was his one true art.

But his regrettably high profile these days meant he was no longer the kind of man who could break into a sheikh's son's London stronghold and expect that to fly beneath the radar. Billionaire philanthropists with celebrity brothers, it turned out, had to follow rules that elite, highly trained soldiers did not. They were expected to use diplomacy and charm.

And if such things were too much of a reach when it concerned an ex-wife rather than a large donation, they were forced to subject themselves to London's gauntlet of "hot spots" and *wait*.

Nikolai checked an impatient sigh, ignoring the squealing trio of underdressed teenagers who leaped up and down in front of him, their eyes dulled with drink, drugs and their own craven self-importance. Lights flashed frenetically, the awful music howled and he monitored the crowd from his strategic position in the shadows of the dance floor.

He simply had to wait for Veronika to show herself, as he knew she would.

Then he would find out how much of what she'd

said seven years ago had been spite, designed to hurt him as much as possible, and how much had been truth. Nikolai knew that on some level, he'd never wanted to know. If he never pressed the issue, then it was always possible that Stefan really *was* his, as Veronika had made him believe for the first five years of the boy's life. That somewhere out there, he had a son. That he had done something right, even if it was by accident.

But such fantasies made him weak, he knew, and he could no longer tolerate it. He wanted a DNA test to prove that Stefan wasn't his. Then he would be done with his weaknesses, once and for all.

"You need to go and fix your life," his brother, Ivan, the only person alive that Nikolai still cared about, the only one who knew what they'd suffered at their uncle's hands in those grim years after their parents had died in a factory fire, had told him just over two years ago. Then he'd stared at Nikolai as if he was a stranger and walked away from him as if he was even less than that.

It was the last time they'd spoken in person, or about anything other than the Korovin Foundation.

Nikolai didn't blame his older brother for this betrayal. He'd watched Ivan's slide into his inevitable madness as it happened. He knew that Ivan was sadly deluded—blinded by sex and emotion, desperate to believe in things that didn't exist because it was far better than the grim alternative of reality. How could he blame Ivan for preferring the delusion? Most people did.

Nikolai didn't have that luxury.

Emotions were liabilities. Lies. Nikolai believed in sex and money. No ties, no temptations. No relationships now his brother had turned his back on him. No possibility that any of the women he took to his bed—always nameless, faceless and only permitted near him if they agreed to adhere to a very strict set of requirements—would ever reach him.

In order to be betrayed, one first had to trust.

And the only person Nikolai had trusted in his life was Ivan and even then, only in a very qualified way once that woman had sunk her claws in him.

But ultimately, this was a gift. It freed him, finally, from his last remaining emotional prison. It made everything simple. Because he had never known how to tell Ivan—who had built a life out of playing the hero in the fighting ring and on the screen, who was able to embody those fights he'd won and the roles he'd played with all the self-righteous fury of the untainted, the unbroken, the *good*—that there were some things that couldn't be fixed.

Nikolai wished he was something so simple as *broken*.

He acted like a man, but was never at risk of becoming one. He'd need flesh and blood, heat and heart for that, and those were the things he'd sold off years ago to make himself into the perfect monster. A killing machine.

Nikolai knew exactly what he was: a bright and shining piece of ice with no hope of warmth, frozen too solid for any sun to penetrate the chill. A hard and deadly weapon, honed to lethal perfection beneath his uncle's fists, then sharpened anew in the bloody Spetsnaz brotherhood. To say nothing of the dark war games he'd learned he could make into his own kind of terrible poetry, despite what it took from him in return.

He was empty where it counted, down to his

bones. Empty all the way through. It was why he was so good at what he did.

And it was safer, Nikolai thought now, his eyes on the heedless, hedonistic crowd. There was too much to lose should he relinquish that deep freeze, give up that iron control. What he remembered of his drinking years appalled him—the blurred nights, the scraps and pieces of too much frustrated emotion turned too quickly into violence, making him far too much like the brutal uncle he'd so despised.

Never again.

It was better by far to stay empty. Cold. Frozen straight through.

He had never been anything but alone. Nikolai understood that now. The truth was, he preferred it that way. And once he dealt with Veronika, once he confirmed the truth about Stefan's paternity, he would never have to be anything else.

Alicia Teller ran out of patience with a sudden jolt, a wave of exhaustion and irritation nearly taking her from her feet in the midst of the jostling crowd. Or possibly that was the laddish group to her left, all of them obviously deep into the night's drinking and therefore flailing around the dance floor.

I'm much too old for this, she told herself as she moved out of their way for the tenth time, feeling ancient and decrepit at her extraordinarily advanced age of twenty-nine.

She couldn't remember the last time she'd spent a Saturday night anywhere more exciting than a quiet restaurant with friends, much less in a slick, pretentious club that had recently been dubbed *the* place to be seen in London. But then again, she also didn't like to look a gift horse in the mouth—said gift horse, in this case, being her ever-exuberant best friend and flatmate Rosie, who'd presented the guest passes to this velvet-roped circus with a grand flourish over dinner.

"It's the coolest place in London right now," she'd confidently assured Alicia over plates of *saag paneer* in their favorite Indian restaurant not far from Brick Lane. "Dripping with celebrities and therefore every attractive man in London."

"I am not cool, Rosie," Alicia had reminded her gently. "You've said so yourself for years. Every single time you try to drag me to yet another club you claim will change my life, if memory serves.

It might be time for you to accept the possibility that this is who I am."

"Never!" Rosie had cried at once, feigning shock and outrage. "I remember when you were *fun,* Alicia. I've made a solemn vow to corrupt you, no matter how long it takes!"

"I'm incorruptible," Alicia had assured her. Because she also remembered when she'd been *fun,* and she had no desire to repeat those terrible mistakes, thank you, much less that descent into shame and heartache. "I'm also very likely to embarrass you. Can you handle the shame?"

Rosie had rolled her extravagantly mascaraed and shimmery-purple shadowed eyes while tossing the last of the poppadoms into her mouth.

"I can handle it," she'd said. "Anything to remind you that you're in your twenties, not your sixties. I consider it a public service."

"You say that," Alicia had teased her, "but you should be prepared for me to request 'Dancing Queen' as if we're at a wedding disco. From the no doubt world-renowned and tragically hip DJ who will faint dead away at the insult."

"Trust me, Alicia," Rosie had said then, very

seriously. "This is going to be the best night of our lives."

Now Alicia watched her best friend shake her hips in a sultry come-on to the investment banker she'd been flirting with all night, and blamed the jet lag. Nothing else could have made her forget for even a moment that sparkly, dramatic still Rosie viewed it as her sacred obligation to pull on a weekend night, the way they both had when they were younger and infinitely wilder, and that meant the exorbitant taxi fare back home from the wilds of this part of East London to the flat they shared on the outskirts of Hammersmith would be Alicia's to cough up. Alone.

"You know what you need?" Rosie had asked on the chilly trek over from the Tube, right on cue. "Desperately, I might add?"

"I know what *you* think I need, yes," Alicia had replied dryly. "But for some reason, the fantasy of sloppy and unsatisfying sex with some stranger from a club pales in comparison to the idea of getting a good night's sleep all alone in my own bed. Call me crazy. Or, barring that, *a grown-up*."

"You're never going to find anyone, you know,"

Rosie had told her then, frowning. "Not if you keep this up. What's next, a nunnery?"

But Alicia knew exactly what kind of people it was possible to meet in the clubs Rosie preferred. She'd met too many of them. She'd *been* one of them throughout her university years. And she'd vowed that she would never, ever let herself get so out of control again. It wasn't worth the price— and sooner or later, there was always a price. In her case, all the years it had taken her to get her father to look at her again.

Alicia had been every inch a Daddy's girl until that terrible night the summer she'd been twenty-one. She'd been indulged and spoiled and adored beyond measure, the light of his life, and she'd lost that forever on a single night she still couldn't piece together in her head. But she knew the details almost as if she could remember it herself, because she'd had to sit and listen to her own father tell them to her the next morning while her head had pounded and her stomach had heaved: she'd been so drunk she'd been practically paralytic when she'd come home that night, but at some point she'd apparently wandered out into the back garden—which was where her father had found her, having sex with Mr. Reddick from next door.

Married Mr. Reddick, with three kids Alicia had babysat over the years, who'd been good mates with her dad until that night. The shame of it was still scarlet in her, bright and horrid, all these years later. How could she have done such a vile, despicable thing? She still didn't know.

Afterward, she'd decided that she'd had more than enough *fun* for one lifetime.

"Sorry," Alicia had said to Rosie then, smiling the painful memories away. "Are you talking about love? I was certain we were talking about the particular desperation of a Saturday night shag...."

"I have a radical idea, Saint Alicia," Rosie had said then with another roll of her eyes toward the dark sky above. "Why don't you put the halo aside for the night? It won't kill you, I promise. You might even find you like a little debauchery on a Saturday night the way you used to do."

Because Rosie didn't know, of course. Nobody knew. Alicia had been too embarrassed, too ashamed, too *disgusted* with herself to tell her friend—to tell anyone—why she'd abruptly stopped going out at the weekend, why she'd thrown herself into the job she hadn't taken seriously until then and turned it into a career she took a great deal of pride in now. Even her mother and sisters didn't know why there had been that sudden deep chill between Alicia and her dad, that had now, years later, only marginally improved into a polite distance.

"I'm not wearing my halo tonight, actually," Alicia had replied primly, patting at her riot of curls as if feeling for one anyway. "It clashed with these shoes you made me wear."

"Idiot," Rosie had said fondly, and then she'd brandished those guest passes and swept them past the crowd outside on the pavement, straight into the clutches of London's hottest club of the moment.

And Alicia had enjoyed herself—more than she'd expected she would, in fact. She'd missed dancing. She'd missed the excitement in the air, the buzz of such a big crowd. The particular, sensual seduction of a good beat. But Rosie's version of fun went on long into the night, the way it always had, and Alicia grew tired too easily. Especially when she'd only flown back into the country the day before, and her body still believed it was in another time zone altogether.

And more, when she wasn't sure she could trust herself. She didn't know what had made her do what she'd done that terrible night eight years ago; she couldn't remember much of it. So she'd opted to avoid anything and everything that might lead down that road—which was easier to do when she wasn't standing in the midst of so much cheerful abandon. Because she didn't have a halo—God knows, she'd proved that with her whorish behavior—she only wished she did.

You knew what this would be like, she thought briskly now, not bothering to fight the banker for Rosie's attention when a text from the backseat of a taxi headed home would do, and would furthermore not cause any interruption to Rosie's obvious plans for the evening. *You could have gone straight home after the curry and sorted out your laundry—*

And then she couldn't help but laugh at herself: Miss Misery Guts acting exactly like the bitter old maid Rosie often darkly intimated she was well on her way to becoming. Rosie was right, clearly. Had she really started thinking about her *laun-*

dry? After midnight on a dance floor in a trendy London club while music even she could tell was fantastic swelled all around her?

Still laughing as she imagined the appalled look Rosie would give her when she told her about this, Alicia turned and began fighting her way out of the wild crowd and off the heaving dance floor. She laughed even harder as she was forced to leap out of the way of a particularly energetic couple flinging themselves here and there.

Alicia overbalanced because she was laughing too hard to pay attention to where she was going, and then, moving too fast to stop herself, she slipped in a puddle of spilled drink on the edge of the dance floor—

And crashed into the dark column of a man that she'd thought, before she hurtled into him, was nothing more than an extension of the speaker behind him. A still, watchful shadow.

He wasn't.

He was hard and male, impossibly muscled, sleek and hot. Alicia's first thought, with her face a scant breath from the most stunning male chest she'd ever beheld in real life and her palms actually *touching* it, was that he smelled like winter—fresh and clean and something deliciously smoky beneath.

She was aware of his hands on her upper arms, holding her fast, and only as she absorbed the fact that he *was* holding her did she also fully comprehend the fact that somehow, despite the press of the crowd and the flashing lights and how quickly she'd been on her way toward taking an undignified header into the floor, he'd managed to catch her at all.

She tilted her head back to thank him for his quick reflexes, still smiling—

And everything stopped.

It simply—*disappeared*.

Alicia felt her heart thud, hard enough to bruise. She felt her mouth drop open.

But she saw nothing at all but his eyes.

Blue like no blue she'd ever seen in another pair of eyes before. Blue like the sky on a crystal cold winter day, so bright it almost hurt to look at him. Blue so intense it seemed to fill her up, expanding inside of her, making her feel swollen with it. As if the slightest thing might make her burst wide-open, and some mad part of her wanted that, desperately.

A touch. A smile. Anything at all.

He was beautiful. Dark and forbidding and still, the most beautiful thing she'd ever seen. Something electric sizzled in the air between them as they gazed at each other, charging through her, making her skin prickle. Making her feel heavy and restless, all at once, as if she was a snow globe he'd picked up and shaken hard, and everything inside of her was still floating drowsily in the air, looking for a place to land.

It scared her, down deep inside in a place she hadn't known was there until this moment—and yet she didn't pull away.

He blinked, as if he felt it too, this terrible, impossible, beautiful thing that crackled between them. She was sure that if she could tear her eyes from his she'd be able to see it there in the air, connecting their bodies, arcing between them and around them and through them, the voltage turned high. The faintest hint of a frown etched between his dark brows, and he moved as if to set her away from him, but then he stopped and all he'd done was shift them both even farther back into the shadows.

And still they stood there, caught. Snared. As

if the world around them, the raucous club, the pounding music, the wild and crazy dancing, had simply evaporated the moment they'd touched.

At last, Alicia thought, in a rush of chaotic sensation and dizzy emotion she didn't understand at all, all of it falling through her with a certain inevitability, like a heavy stone into a terrifyingly deep well.

"My God," she said, gazing up at him. "You look like a wolf."

Was that a smile? His mouth was lush and grim at once, impossibly fascinating to her, and it tugged in one hard corner. Nothing more, and yet she smiled back at him as if he'd beamed at her.

"Is that why you've dressed in red, like a Shoreditch fairy tale?" he asked, his words touched with the faint, velvet caress of an accent she didn't recognize immediately. "I should warn you, it will end with teeth."

"I think you mean tears." She searched his hard face, looking for more evidence of that smile. "It will end in *tears,* surely."

"That, too." Another small tug in the corner of that mouth. "But the teeth usually come first, and hurt more."

"I'll be very disappointed now if you don't have fangs," she told him, and his hands changed their steely grip on her arms, or perhaps she only then became aware of the heat of his palms and how the way he was holding her was so much like a caress.

Another tug on that austere mouth, and an answering one low in her belly, which should have terrified her, given what she knew about herself and sex. On some level, it did.

But she still didn't move away from him.

"It is, of course, my goal in life to keep strange British women who crash into me in crowded clubs from the jaws of disappointment," he said, a new light in his lovely eyes, and a different, more aware tilt to the way he held his head, the way he angled his big body toward her.

As if he might lean in close and swallow her whole.

Staring back at him then, his strong hands hard and hot on her arms and her palms still pressed flat against his taut chest, Alicia wanted nothing more than for him to do exactly that.

She should have turned away then and bolted for the door. Tried to locate whatever was left of her sanity, wherever she'd misplaced it. But she'd never felt this kind of raw, shimmering excitement before, this blistering heat weighing down her limbs so deliciously, this man so primal and powerful she found it hard to breathe.

"Even if the jaws in question are yours?" she asked, and she didn't recognize that teasing lilt in her voice, the way she tilted her head to look up at him, the liquid sort of feeling that moved in her then.

"Especially if they're mine," he replied, his bright winter gaze on her mouth, though there was a darkness there too, a shadow across his intriguing blade of a face that she nearly got lost in. *Jaws,* she reminded herself. *Fangs. He's telling me what a wolf he is, big and bad.* Surely she should feel more alarmed than she did—surely she shouldn't have the strangest urge to soothe him, instead? "You should know there are none sharper or more dangerous."

"In all of London?" She couldn't seem to keep herself from smiling again, or that sparkling cascade of something like light from rushing in her, making her stomach tighten and her breasts pull tight. *Alive. At last.* "Have you measured them, then? Is there some kind of competition you can enter to prove yours are the longest? The sharpest in all the land?"

Alicia felt completely outside herself. Some part of her wanted to lie down in it, in this mad feeling, in *him*—and exult in it. Bask in it as if it was sunshine. As if *he* was, despite the air of casual menace he wore so easily, like an extra layer of skin. Was that visible to everyone, or only to her? She didn't care. She wanted to roll around in this moment, in him, like it was the first snow of the season and she could make it all into angels.

Her breath caught at the image, and somehow, he heard it. She felt his reaction in the sudden tension of his powerful frame above her and around her, in the flex of his fingers high on her arms, in the tightening of that connection that wound between them, bright and electric, and made her feel like a stranger in her own body.

His blue eyes lifted to meet hers and gleamed bright. "I don't need to measure them, *solnyshka*." He shifted closer, and his attention returned to her mouth. "I know."

He was an arctic wolf turned man, every inch of him a predator—lean and hard as he stood over her despite the heels Rosie had coerced her into wearing. He wore all black, a tight black T-shirt beneath a perfectly tailored black jacket, dark trousers and boots, and his wide, hard shoulders made her skin feel tight. His dark hair was short and inky black. It made his blue eyes seem like smoke over his sculpted jaw and cheekbones, and yet all of it, all of *him,* was hard and male and so dangerous she could feel it hum beneath her skin, some part of her desperate to fight, to flee. He looked intriguingly uncivilized. Something like feral.

And yet Alicia wasn't afraid, as that still-alarmed, still-vigilant part of her knew she should have been. Not when he was looking at her like that. Not when she followed a half-formed instinct and moved closer to him, pressing her hands flatter against the magnificently formed planes of his chest while his arms went around her to hold her like a lover might. She tilted her head back even farther and watched his eyes turn to arctic fire.

She didn't understand it, but she burned.

This isn't right, a small voice cautioned her in the back of her mind. *This isn't you.*

But he was so beautiful she couldn't seem to

keep track of who she was supposed to be, and her heart hurt her where it thundered in her chest. She felt something bright and demanding knot into an insistent ache deep in her belly, and she found she couldn't think of a good reason to step away from him.

In a minute, she promised herself. *I'll walk away in a minute.*

"You should run," he told her then, his voice dark and low, and she could see he was serious. That he meant it. But one of his hands moved to trace a lazy pattern on her cheek as he said it, his palm a rough velvet against her skin, and she shivered. His blue gaze seemed to sharpen. "As far away from me as you can get."

He looked so grim then, so sure, and it hurt her, somehow. She wanted to see him smile with that hard, dangerous mouth. She wanted that with every single part of her and she didn't even know his name.

None of this made any sense.

Alicia had been so good for so long. She'd paid and paid and paid for that single night eight years ago. She'd been so vigilant, so careful, ever since. She was never spontaneous. She was never reckless. And yet this beautiful shadow of a man had the bluest eyes she'd ever seen, and the saddest mouth, and the way he touched her made her shake and burn and glow.

And she thought that maybe this once, for a moment or two, she could let down her guard. Just the smallest, tiniest bit. It didn't have to mean anything she didn't want it to mean. It didn't have to mean anything at all.

So she ignored that voice inside of her, and she ignored his warning, too.

Alicia leaned her face into his hard palm as if it was the easiest thing in the world, and smiled when he pulled in a breath like it was a fire in him, too. Like he felt the same burn.

She stretched up against his hard, tough body and told herself this was about that grim mouth of his, not the wild, impossible things she knew she shouldn't let herself feel or want or, God help her, *do*. And they were in the shadows of a crowded club where nobody could see her and no one would ever know what she did in the dark. It wasn't as if it counted.

She could go back to her regularly scheduled quiet life in a moment.

It would only be a moment. One small moment outside all the rules she'd made for herself, the rules she'd lived by so carefully for so long, and then she would go straight back home to her neat, orderly, virtuous life.

She would. She had to. *She would.*

But first Alicia obeyed that surge of wild demand inside of her, leaned closer and fitted her mouth to his.

CHAPTER TWO

HE TASTED LIKE the night. Better even than she'd imagined.

He paused for the barest instant when Alicia's lips touched his. Half a heartbeat. Less.

A scant second while the taste of him seared through her, deep and dark and wild. She thought that was enough, that small taste of his fascinating mouth. That would do, and now she could go back to her quiet—

But then he angled his head to one side, used the hand at her cheek to guide her mouth where he wanted it and took over.

Devouring her like the wolf she understood he was. *He really was,* and the realization swirled inside of her like heat. His mouth was impossibly carnal, opening over hers to taste her, to claim her.

Dark and deep, hot and sure.

Alicia simply…exploded. It was like a long flash of light, shuddering and bright, searing everything away in the white hot burn of it. It was perfect. It was beautiful.

It was too much.

She shivered against him, overloaded with his bold taste, the scrape of his jaw, his talented fingers moving her mouth where he wanted it in a silent, searing command she was happy to obey. Then his hands were in her hair, buried in her thick curls. Her arms went around his neck of their own volition, and then she was plastered against the tall, hard length of him. It was like pressing into the surface of the sun and still, she couldn't seem to get close enough.

As if there was no *close enough*.

And he kissed her, again and again, with a ruthless intensity that made her feel weak and beautiful all at once, until she was mindless with need. Until she forgot her own name. Until she forgot she didn't know his. Until she forgot how dangerous *forgetting* was for her.

Until she forgot everything but him.

When he pulled back, she didn't understand. He put an inch, maybe two, between them, and then he muttered something harsh and incomprehensible while he stared at her as if he thought she was some kind of ghost.

It took her a long, confused moment to realize that she couldn't understand him because he wasn't speaking in English, not because she'd forgotten her own language, too.

Alicia blinked, the world rushing back as she did. She was still standing in that club. Music still pounded all around them, lights still flashed, well-dressed patrons still shouted over the din, and somewhere out in the middle of the dance floor, Rosie was no doubt still playing her favorite game with her latest conquest.

Everything was as it had been before she'd stumbled into this man, before he'd caught her. Before she'd kissed him.

Before he'd kissed her back.

Everything was exactly the same. Except Alicia.

He was searching her face as if he was looking for something. He shook his head slightly, then reached down and ran a lazy finger over the ridge of her collarbone, as if testing its shape. Even that made her shudder, that simple slide of skin against skin. Even so innocuous a touch seemed directly connected to that pulsing heat between her legs, the heavy ache in her breasts, the hectic spin inside of her.

She didn't have to speak his language to know whatever he muttered then was a curse.

If she were smart, the way she'd tried to be for years now, she would pull her hand away and run. Just as he'd told her she should. Just as she'd promised herself she would. Everything about this was too extreme, too intense, as if he wasn't only a strange man in a club but the kind of drug that usually went with this kind of rolling, wildly out-of-control feeling. As if she was much too close to being high on *him*.

"Last chance," he said then, as if he could read her mind.

He was giving her a warning. Again.

In her head, she listened. She smiled politely and extricated herself. She marched herself to the nearest exit, hailed a taxi, then headed straight home to the comfort of her bloody laundry. Because she knew she couldn't be trusted outside the confines of the rules she'd made for herself. She'd been living the consequences of having no rules for a long, long time.

But here, now, in this loud place surrounded by

so many people and all of that pounding music, she didn't feel like the person she'd been when she'd arrived. Everything she knew about herself had twisted inside out. Turned into something else entirely in that electric blue of his challenging gaze.

As if this really was a Shoreditch fairy tale, after all.

"What big eyes you have," she teased him.

His hard mouth curved then, and she felt it like a burst of heat, like sunlight. She couldn't do anything but smile back at him.

"So be it," he said, as if he despaired of them both.

Alicia laughed, then laughed again at the startled look in his eyes.

"The dourness is a lovely touch," she told him. "You must be beating them off with a stick. A very grim stick."

"No stick," he said, in an odd tone. "A look at me is usually sufficient."

"A wolf," she said, and grinned. "Just as I suspected."

He blinked, and again looked at her in that strange way of his, as if she was an apparition he couldn't quite believe was standing there before him.

Then he moved with the same decisiveness he'd used when he'd taken control of that kiss, tucking her into his side as he navigated his way through the dense crowd. She tried not to think about how well she fitted there, under his heavy arm, tight against the powerful length of his torso as he cut through the crowd. She tried not to drift away in the scent of him, the heat and the power, all of it surrounding her and pouring into that ache already inside of her, making it bloom and stretch and grow.

Until it took over everything.

Maybe she was under some kind of spell, Alicia thought with the small part of her that wasn't consumed with the feel of his tall, lean frame as he guided her so protectively through the crowd. It should have been impossible to move through the club so quickly, so confidently. Not in a place like this at the height of a Saturday night. But he did it.

And then they were outside, in the cold and the damp November night, and he was still moving in that same breathtaking way, like quicksilver. Like he knew exactly where they were headed—away from the club and the people still milling about in front of it. He led her down the dark street, deeper into the shadows, and it was then Alicia's sense of self-preservation finally kicked itself into gear.

Better late than never, she thought, annoyed with herself, but it actually *hurt* her to pull away from the magnificent shelter of his body, from all of that intense heat and strength. It felt like she'd ripped her skin off when she stepped away from him, as if they'd been fused together.

He regarded her calmly, making her want to trust him when she knew she shouldn't. She couldn't.

"I'm sorry, but..." She wrapped her arms around her own waist in an attempt to make up for the heat she'd lost when she'd stepped away from him. "I don't know a single thing about you."

"You know several things, I think."

He sounded even more delicious now that they were alone and she could hear him properly. *Russian,* she thought, as pleased as if she'd learned his deepest, darkest secrets.

"Yes," she agreed, thinking of the things she knew. Most of them to do with that insistent ache

in her belly, and lower. His mouth. His clever
hands. "All lovely things. But none of them worth
risking my personal safety for, I'm sure you'll
agree."

Something like a smile moved in his eyes, but
didn't make it to his hard mouth. Still, it echoed
in her, sweet and light, making her feel far more
buoyant than she should have on a dark East London street with a strange man even she could see
was dangerous, no matter how much she wanted
him.

Had she ever wanted anything this much? Had
anyone?

"A wolf is never without risk," he told her, that
voice of his like whiskey, smooth and scratchy at
once, heating her up from the inside out. "That's
the point of wolves. Or you'd simply get a dog,
pat it on the head." His eyes gleamed. "Teach it
tricks."

Alicia wasn't sure she wanted to know the tricks
this man had up his sleeve. Or, more to the point,
she wasn't sure she'd survive them. She wasn't
certain she'd survive this as it was.

"You could be very bad in bed," she said, conversationally, as if she picked up strange men all

the time. She hardly recognized her own light, easy, flirtatious tone. She hadn't heard it since before that night in her parents' back garden. "That's a terrible risk to take with any stranger, and awkward besides."

That smile in his eyes intensified, got even bluer. "I'm not."

She believed him.

"You could be the sort who gets very, very drunk and weeps loudly about his broken heart until dawn." She gave a mock shudder. "So tedious, especially if poetry is involved. Or worse, *singing*."

"I don't drink," he countered at once. His dark brows arched over those eyes of his, challenging her. Daring her. "I never sing, I don't write poems and I certainly do not weep." He paused. "More to the point, I don't have a heart."

"Handy, that," she replied easily. She eyed him. "You could be a killer, of course. That would be unfortunate."

She smiled at that. He didn't.

"And if I am?"

"There you go," she said, and nodded sagely.

Light, airy. Enchanted, despite herself. "I can't possibly go off into the night with you now, can I?"

But it was terrifying how much she *wanted* to go off with him, wherever he'd take her, and instead of reacting to that as she should, she couldn't stop smiling at him. As if she already knew him, this strange man dressed all in black, his blue eyes the only spot of color on the cold pavement as he stared at her as if she'd stunned him somehow.

"My name is Nikolai," he said, and she had the oddest impression he hadn't meant to speak at all. He shifted, then reached over and traced her lips with his thumb, his expression so fierce, so intent, it made her feel hollowed out inside, everything scraped away except that wild, wondrous heat he stirred in her. "Text someone my name and address. Have them ring every fifteen minutes if you like. Send the police. Whatever you want."

"All those safeguards are very thoughtful," she pointed out, but her eyes felt too wide and her voice sounded insubstantial. Wispy. "Though not exactly wolfish, it has to be said."

His mouth moved into his understated version of a smile

"I want you." His eyes were on fire. Every inch of him that wolf. "What will it take?"

She swayed back into him as if they were magnets and she'd simply succumbed to the pull. And then she had no choice but to put her hand to his abdomen, to feel all that blasting heat right there beneath her palm.

Even that didn't scare her the way it should.

"What big teeth you have," she whispered, too on edge to laugh, too filled with that pulsing ache inside of her to smile.

"The biting part comes later." His eyes gleamed again, with the kind of sheer male confidence that made it difficult to breathe. Alicia stopped trying. "If you ask nicely."

He picked up her hand and lifted it to his mouth, tracing a dark heat over the back of it. He didn't look away.

"If you're sure," she said piously, trying desperately to pretend she wasn't shaking, and that he couldn't feel it. That he didn't know exactly what he was doing to her when she could see full well that he did. "I was promised a wolf, not a dog."

"I eat dogs for breakfast."

She laughed then. "That's not particularly comforting."

"I can't be what I'm not, *solnyshka*." He turned her hand over, then kissed her palm in a way that made her hiss in a sharp breath. His eyes were smiling again, so bright and blue. "But I'm very good at what I am."

And she'd been lost since she'd set eyes on him, hadn't she? What use was there in pretending otherwise? She wasn't drunk. It wasn't like that terrible night, because she knew what she was doing. Didn't she?

"Note to self," Alicia managed to say, breathless and dizzy and unable to remember why she'd tried to stop this in the first place, when surrendering to it—to him—felt so much like triumph. Like fate. "Never eat breakfast with a wolf. The sausages are likely the family dog."

He shrugged. "Not *your* family dog," he said with that fierce mouth of his, though she was sure his blue eyes laughed. "If that helps."

And this time, when she smiled at him, the negotiation was over.

The address he gave her in his clipped, direct way was in an extraordinarily posh part of town

Alicia could hardly afford to visit, much less live in. She dutifully texted it to Rosie, hoping that her friend was far too busy to check it until morning. And then she tucked her phone away and forgot about Rosie altogether.

Because he still moved like magic, tucking her against him again as if there was a crowd he needed to part when there was only the late-night street and what surged between them like heat lightning. As if he liked the way she fitted there as much as she did. And her heart began to pound all over again, excitement and anticipation and a certain astonishment at her own behavior pouring through her with every hard thump.

At the corner, he lifted his free hand almost languidly toward the empty street, and for a second Alicia truly believed that he was so powerful that taxis simply materialized before him at his whim—until a nearby engine turned over and a powerful black SUV slid out of the shadows and pulled to a stop right there before them.

More magic, when she was enchanted already.

Nikolai, she whispered to herself as she climbed inside the SUV, as if the name was a song. Or a spell. *His name is Nikolai.*

He swung in behind her on the soft leather back-seat, exchanged a few words in curt Russian with the driver and then pressed a button that raised a privacy shield, secluding them. Then he settled back against the seat, near her but not touching her, stretching out his long, lean body and making the spacious vehicle seem tight. Close.

And then he simply looked at her.

As if he was trying to puzzle her out. Or giving her one last chance to bolt.

But Alicia knew she wasn't going to do that.

"More talk of dogs?" he asked mildly, yet all she heard was the hunger beneath. She could see it in his eyes, his face. She could feel the echo of it in her, new and huge and almost more than she could bear. "More clever little character assessments couched as potential objections?"

"I got in your car," she pointed out, hardly recognizing her own voice. The thick heat in it. "I think I'm done."

He smiled. She was sure of it, though his mouth didn't move. But she could see the stamp of satisfaction on his hard face, the flare of a deep male approval.

"Not yet, *solnyshka,*" he murmured, his voice a low rasp. "Not quite yet."

And she melted. It was a shivery thing, hot and desperate, like she couldn't quite catch her breath against the heat of it.

"Come here," he said.

They were cocooned in the darkness, light spilling here and there as the car sped through the city, and still his blue gaze was brilliant. Compelling. And so knowing—so certain of himself, of her, of what was about to happen—it made her blood run hot in her veins.

Alicia didn't move fast enough and he made a low noise. *A growl*—like the wolf he so resembled. The rough sound made her shake apart and then melt down into nothing but need, alive with that crazy heat she couldn't seem to control any longer.

He simply picked her up and pulled her into his lap, his mouth finding hers and claiming her all over again with an impatience that delighted her. She met him with the same urgency. His hands marveled down the length of her back, explored the shape of her hips, and Alicia's mind blanked out into a red-hot burst of that consuming, impossible fire. Into pure and simple *need*.

It had been so long. *So long,* and yet her body knew exactly what to do, thrilling to the taste of him, the feel of his hard, capable hands first over and then underneath her bright red shirt. His hands on her stomach, her waist, her breasts. So perfect she wanted to die. And not nearly enough.

He leaned back to peel off his jacket and the tight black T-shirt beneath, and her eyes glazed over at the sight of all of that raw male beauty. She pressed herself against the hard planes of his perfect chest, tracing the large, colorful tattoos that stretched over his skin with trembling fingers, with her lips and her tongue, tasting art etched across art.

Intense. Hot. Intoxicating.

And that scent of his—of the darkest winter, smoke and ice—surrounded her. Licked into her. Claimed her as surely as he did.

One moment she was fully clothed, the next her shirt and the bra beneath it were swept away, while his hard mouth took hers again and again until she thought she might die if he stopped. Then he did stop, and she moaned out her distress, her desperation. That needy ache so deep in the core of her. But he only laughed softly, before he fastened his hot mouth to the tight peak of one breast and sucked on it, not quite gently, until she thought she really *had* died.

The noises she heard herself making were impossible. Nothing could really feel this good. This perfect. This wild or this *right*.

Nikolai shifted, lifting her, and Alicia helped him peel her trousers down from her hips, kicking one leg free and not caring what happened to the other. She felt outside herself and yet more fully *in* herself than she had been in as long as she could remember. She explored the expanse of his gorgeous shoulders, the distractingly tender spot behind his ear, the play of his stunning muscles, perfectly honed beneath her.

He twisted them both around, coming down over her on the seat and pulling her legs around his hips with an urgency that made her breath desert her. She hadn't even been aware that he'd undressed. It was more magic—and then he was finally naked against her, the steel length of him a hot brand against her belly.

Alicia shuddered and melted, then melted again,

and he moved even closer, one of his hands moving to her bottom and lifting her against him with that devastating skill, that easy mastery, that made her belly tighten.

He was muttering in Russian, that same word he'd used before like a curse or a prayer or even both at once, and the sound of it made her moan again. It was harsh like him, and tender, too. It made her feel as if she might come out of her own skin. He teased her breasts, licking his way from one proud nipple to the other as if he might lose himself there, then moved to her neck, making her shiver against him before he took her mouth again in a hard, deep kiss.

As raw as she was. As undone.

He pulled back slightly to press something into her hand, and she blinked at it, taking much longer than she should have to recognize it was the condom she hadn't thought about for even an instant.

A trickle of unease snaked down the back of her neck, but she pushed it away, too far gone for shame. Not when his blue eyes glittered with sensual intent and his long fingers moved between them, feeling her damp heat and then stroking deep into her molten center, making her clench him hard.

"Hurry," he told her.

"I'm hurrying. You're distracting me."

He played his fingers in and out of her, slick and hot, then pressed the heel of his hand into her neediest part, laughing softly when she bucked against him.

"Concentrate, *solnyshka*."

She ripped open the foil packet, then took her time rolling it down his velvety length, until he cursed beneath his breath.

Alicia liked the evidence of his own pressing need. She liked that she could make his breath catch, too. And then he stopped, braced over her, his face close to hers and the hardest part of him poised at her entrance but not *quite*—

He groaned. He sounded as tortured as she felt. She liked that, too.

"Your name."

She blinked at the short command, so gruff and harsh. His arms were hard around her, his big body pressed her back into the soft leather seat, and she felt delicate and powerful all at once.

"Tell me your name," he said, nipping at her jaw,

making her head fall back to give him any access he desired, anything he wanted.

Alive, she thought again. *At last.*

"Alicia," she whispered.

He muttered it like a fierce prayer, and then he thrust into her—hot and hard and so perfect, so beautiful, that tears spilled from her eyes even as she shattered around him.

"Again," he said.

It was another command, arrogant and darkly certain. Nikolai was hard and dangerous and between her legs, his eyes bright and hot and much too intense on hers. She turned her head away but he caught her mouth with his, taking her over, conquering her.

"I don't think I can—" she tried to say against his mouth, even while the flames still licked through her, even as she still shuddered helplessly around him, aware of the steel length of him inside her, filling her.

Waiting.

That hard smile like a burst of heat inside her. "You will."

And then he started to move.

It was perfect. More than perfect. It was sleek

and hot, impossibly good. He simply claimed her, took her, and Alicia met him. She arched into him, lost in the slide and the heat, the glory of it. Of him.

Slick. Wild.

Perfect.

He moved in her, over her, his mouth at her neck and his hands roaming from her bottom to the center of her shuddering need as he set the wild, intense pace. She felt it rage inside her again, this mad fire she'd never felt before and worried would destroy her even as she hungered for more. And more. *And more.*

She met every deep thrust. She gloried in it.

"Say my name," he said, gruff against her ear, his voice washing through her and sending her higher, making her glow. "Now, Alicia. Say it."

When she obeyed he shuddered, then let out another low, sexy growl that moved over her like a newer, better fire. He reached between them and pressed down hard against the heart of her hunger, hurtling her right over the edge again.

And smiled, she was sure of it, with his warrior's mouth as well as those winter-bright eyes, right before he followed her into bliss.

* * *

Nikolai came back to himself with a vicious, jarring thud.

He couldn't move. He wasn't sure he breathed. Alicia quivered sweetly beneath him, his mouth was pressed against the tender junction of her neck and shoulder, and he was still deep inside her lovely body.

What the hell was that?

He shifted her carefully into the seat beside him, ignoring the way her long, inky-black lashes looked against the creamy brown of her skin, the way her perfect, lush mouth was so soft now. He ignored the tiny noise she made in the back of her throat, as if distressed to lose contact with him, which made him grit his teeth. But she didn't open her eyes.

He dealt with the condom swiftly, then he found his trousers in the tangle of clothes on the floor of the car and jerked them on. He had no idea what had happened to his T-shirt, and decided it didn't matter. And then he simply sat there as if he was winded.

He, Nikolai Korovin, *winded.* By a woman.

By *this* woman.

What moved in him then was like a rush of too many colors, brilliant and wild, when he knew the only safety lay in gray. It surged in his veins, it pounded in his temples, it scraped along his sex. He told himself it was temper, but he knew better. It was everything he'd locked away for all these years, and he didn't want it. He wouldn't allow it. It made him feel like an animal again, wrong and violent and insane and drunk....

That was it.

It rang like a bell in him, low and urgent, swelling into everything. Echoing everywhere. No wonder he felt so off-kilter, so dangerously unbalanced. This woman made him feel *drunk*.

Nikolai forced a breath, then another.

Everything that had happened since she'd tripped in front of him flashed through his head, in the same random snatches of color and sound and scent he remembered from a thousand morning-afters. Her laughter, that sounded the way he thought joy must, though he'd no basis for comparison. The way she'd tripped and then fallen, straight into him, and hadn't had the sense to roll herself as he would have done, to break her fall.

Her brilliant smile that cracked over her face so easily. Too easily.

No one had ever smiled at him like that. As if he was a real man. Even a good one.

But he knew what he was. He'd always known. His uncle's fists, worse after Ivan had left to fight their way to freedom one championship at a time. The things he'd done in the army. Veronika's calculated deception, even Ivan's more recent betrayal—these had only confirmed what Nikolai had always understood to be true about himself down deep into his core.

To think differently now, when he'd lost everything he had to lose and wanted nothing more than to shut himself off for good, was the worst kind of lie. Damaging. Dangerous. And he knew what happened when he allowed himself to become intoxicated. How many times would he have to prove that to himself? How many people would he hurt?

He was better off blank. Ice cold and gray, all the way through.

The day after Veronika left him, Nikolai had woken bruised and battered from another fight—or *fights*—he couldn't recall. He'd been shaky.

Sick from the alcohol and sicker still with himself. Disgusted with the holes in his memory and worse, with all the things he *did* remember. The things that slid without context through his head, oily and barbed.

His fists against flesh. His bellow of rage. The crunch of wood beneath his foot, the shattering of pottery against the stone floor. Faces of strangers on the street, wary. Worried. Then angry. Alarmed.

Blood on a fist—and only some of it his. *Fear in those eyes*—never his. Nikolai was what grown men feared, what they crossed streets to avoid, but he hadn't felt fear himself in years. Not since he'd been a child.

Fear meant there was something left to lose.

That was the last time Nikolai had drunk a drop of alcohol and it was the last time he'd let himself lose control.

Until now.

He didn't understand this. He was not an impulsive man. He didn't pick up women, he *picked* them, carefully—and only when he was certain that whatever else they were, they were obedient and disposable.

When they posed no threat to him at all. Nikolai breathed in, out.

He'd survived wars. This was only a woman.

Nikolai looked at her then, memorizing her, like
she was a code he needed to crack, instead of the
bomb itself, poised to detonate.

She wore her dark black hair in a cloud of tight
curls around her head, a tempting halo around her
lovely, clever face, and he didn't want any part of
this near-overpowering desire that surged in him,
to bury his hands in the heavy thickness of it, to
start the wild rush all over again. Her body was
lithe and ripe with warm, mouthwatering curves
that he'd already touched and tasted, so why did
he feel as if it had all been rushed, as if it wasn't
nearly enough?

He shouldn't have this longing to take his time,
to really explore her. He shouldn't hunger for that
lush, full mouth of hers again, or want to taste his
way along that elegant neck for the simple pleasure of making her shiver. He shouldn't find it so
impossible to look at her without imagining himself tracing lazy patterns across every square inch
of the sweet brown perfection of her skin. With

his mouth and then his hands, again and again until he *knew* her.

He'd asked her name, as if he'd needed it. He'd wanted her that much, and Nikolai knew better than to want. It could only bring him pain.

Vodka had been his one true love, and it had ruined him. It had let loose that monster in him, let it run amok. It had taken everything that his childhood and the army hadn't already divided between them and picked down to the bone. He'd known it in his sober moments, but he hadn't cared. Because vodka had warmed him, lent color and volume to the dark, silent prison of his life, made him imagine he could be something other than a six-foot-two column of glacial ice.

But he knew better than that now. He knew better than this.

Alicia's eyes fluttered open then, dark brown shot through with amber, almost too pretty to bear. He hated that he noticed, that he couldn't look away. She glanced around as if she'd forgotten where they were. Then she looked at him.

She didn't smile that outrageously beautiful smile of hers, and it made something hitch inside him, like a stitch in his side. As if he'd lost that, too.

She lifted one foot, shaking her head at the trousers that were still attached to her ankle, and the shoe she'd never removed. She reached down, picked up the tangle of her bright red shirt and lacy pink bra from the pile on the floor of the car, and sighed.

And Nikolai relaxed, because he was back on familiar ground.

Now came the demands, the negotiations, he thought cynically. The endless manipulations, which were the reason he'd started making any woman who wanted him agree to his rules before he touched her. Sign the appropriate documents, understand exactly how this would go before it started. Nikolai knew this particular dance well. It was why he normally didn't pick up women, let them into the sleek, muscular SUV that told them too much about his net worth, much less give them his address....

But instead of pouting prettily and pointedly, almost always the first transparent step in these situations, Alicia looked at him, let her head fall back and laughed.

CHAPTER THREE

THAT DAMNED LAUGH.

Nikolai would rather be shot again, he decided in that electric moment as her laughter filled the car. He would rather take another knife or two to the gut. He didn't know what on earth he was supposed to do with laughter like that, when it sparkled in the air all around him and fell indiscriminately here and there, like a thousand unwelcome caresses all over his skin and something worse—much worse—deep beneath it.

He scowled.

"Never let it be said this wasn't classy," Alicia said, her lovely voice wry. "I suppose we'll always have that going for us."

There was no we. There was no *us*. Neither of those words were *disposable*. Alarms shrieked like air raid sirens inside of him, mixing with the aftereffects of that laugh.

"I thought you understood," he said abruptly, at his coldest and most cutting. "I don't—"

"Relax, Tin Man." Laughter still lurked in her voice. She tugged her trousers back up over her hips, then pulled her bra free of her shirt, shooting him a breezy smile that felt not unlike a blade to the stomach as she clipped it back into place. "I heard you the first time. No heart."

And then she ignored him, as if he wasn't vibrating beside her with all of that darkness and icy intent. As if he wasn't Nikolai Korovin, feared and respected in equal measure all across the planet, in a thousand corporate boardrooms as well as the grim theaters of too many violent conflicts. As if he was the kind of man someone could simply *pick up* in a London club and then dismiss...

Except, of course, he was. Because she had. She'd done exactly that.

He'd let her.

Alicia fussed with her shirt before pulling it over her head, her black curls springing out of the opening in a joyful froth that made him actually ache to touch them. *Her.* He glared down at his hands as if they'd betrayed him.

When she looked at him again, her dark

eyes were soft, undoing him as surely as if she really had eviscerated him with a hunting knife. He would have preferred the latter. She made it incalculably worse by reaching over and smoothing her warm hand over his cheek, offering him... comfort?

"You look like you've swallowed broken glass," she said.

Kindly.

Very much as if she cared.

Nikolai didn't want what he couldn't have. It had been beaten out of him long ago. It was a simple, unassailable fact, like gravity. Like air.

Like light.

But he couldn't seem to stop himself from lifting his hand, tracing that tempting mouth of hers once more, watching the heat bloom again in her eyes.

Just one night, he told himself then. He couldn't help it. That smile of hers made him realize he was so tired of the cold, the dark. That he felt haunted by the things he'd lost, the wars he'd won, the battles he'd been fighting all his life. Just once, he *wanted.*

One night to explore this light of hers she shone

so indiscriminately, he thought. Just one night to pretend he was something more than ice. A wise man didn't step onto a land mine when he could see it lying there in front of him, waiting to blow. But Nikolai had been through more hells than he could count. He could handle anything for a night. Even this. Even her.

Just one night.

"You should hold on," he heard himself say. He slid his hand around to cup the nape of her neck, and exulted in the shiver that moved over her at even so small a touch. As if she was his. That could never happen, he knew. But he'd allowed himself the night. He had every intention of making it a long one. "I'm only getting started."

If only he really had been a wolf.

Alicia scowled down at the desk in her office on Monday and tried valiantly to think of something—*anything*—other than Nikolai. And failed, as she'd been doing with alarming regularity since she'd sneaked away from his palatial penthouse in South Kensington early on Sunday morning.

If he'd really been a wolf, she'd likely be in hospital right now, recovering from being bitten in a lovely quiet coma or restful medicated haze, which would mean she'd be enjoying a much-needed holiday from the self-recriminating clamor inside her head.

At least I wasn't drunk....

Though if she was honest, some part of her almost wished she had been. *Almost.* As if that would be some kind of excuse when she knew from bitter experience that it wasn't.

The real problem was, she'd been perfectly aware of what she was doing on Saturday. She'd gone ahead and done it precisely *because* she hadn't been drunk. For no other reason than that she'd wanted him.

From her parents' back garden to a stranger in a car. She hadn't learned much of anything in all these years, had she? Given the chance, she'd glee-fully act the promiscuous whore—drunk *or* sober.

That turned inside of her like bile, acidic and thick at the back of her throat.

"I think you must be a witch," he'd said at some point in those long, sleepless hours of too much pleasure, too hot and too addicting. He'd been sprawled out next to her, his rough voice no more than a growl in the dark of his cavernous bedroom.

A girl could get lost in a room like that, she'd thought. In a bed so wide. In a man like Nikolai, who had taken her over and over with a skill and a thoroughness and a sheer masculine prowess that made her wonder how she'd ever recover from it. *If* she would. But she hadn't wanted to think those things, not then. Not while it was still dark outside and they were cocooned on those soft sheets together, the world held at bay. There'd be time enough to work on forgetting, she'd thought. When it was over.

When it was morning.

She'd propped herself up on an elbow and looked down at him, his bold, hard face in shadows but those eyes of his as intense as ever.

"I'm not the driving force in this fairy tale," she'd said quietly. Then she'd dropped her gaze lower, past that hard mouth of his she now knew was a terrible, electric torment when he chose, and down to that astonishing torso of his laid out before her like a feast. "Red Riding Hood is a hapless little fool, isn't she? Always in the wrong place at the wrong time."

Alicia had meant that to come out light and breezy, but it hadn't. It had felt intimate instead, somehow. Darker and deeper, and a different kind of ache inside. Not at all what she'd intended.

She'd felt the blue of his gaze like a touch.

Instead of losing herself there, she'd traced a lazy finger over the steel plates of his harshly honed chest. Devastatingly perfect. She moved from this scar to that tattoo, tracing each pucker of flesh, each white strip of long-ago agony, then smoothing her fingertip over the bright colors and Cyrillic letters that flowed everywhere else. Two kinds of marks, stamped permanently into his flesh. She'd been uncertain if she was fascinated or something else, something that made her mourn for all his body had suffered.

But it wasn't her place to ask.

"Bullet," he'd said quietly, when her fingers moved over a slightly raised and shiny patch of skin below his shoulder, as if she had asked after all. "I was in the army."

"For how long?"

"Too long."

She'd flicked a look at him, but had kept going, finding a long, narrow white scar that slashed across his taut abdomen and following the length of it, back and forth. So much violence boiled down to a thin white line etched into his hard, smooth flesh. It had made her hurt for him, but she still hadn't asked.

"Kitchen knife. My uncle." His voice had been little more than a rasp against the dark. She'd gone still, her fingers splayed across the scar in question. "He took his role as our guardian seriously," Nikolai had said, and his gruff voice had sounded almost amused, as if what he'd said was something other than awful. Alicia had chanced a glance at him, and saw a different truth in that wintry gaze, more vulnerable in the clasp of the dark than she'd imagined he knew. "He didn't like how I'd washed the dishes."

"Nikolai—" she'd begun, not knowing what she could possibly say, but spurred on by that torn look in his eyes.

He'd blinked, then frowned. "It was nothing."

But she'd known he was lying. And the fact that she'd had no choice but to let it pass, that this man wasn't hers to care for no matter how it felt as if he should have been, had rippled through her like actual, physical pain.

Alicia had moved on then to the tattoo of a wild beast rendered in a shocking sweep of bold color and dark black lines that wrapped around the left side of his body, from his shoulder all the way down to an inch or so above his sex. It was fierce and furious, all ferocious teeth and wicked claws, poised there as if ready to devour him.

As if, she'd thought, it already had.

"All of my sins," he'd said then, his voice far darker and rougher than before.

There'd been an almost-guarded look in his winter gaze when she'd glanced up at him, but she'd thought that was that same vulnerability again. And then he'd sucked in a harsh breath when she'd leaned over and pressed a kiss to the fearsome head of this creature that claimed him, as if she could wash away the things that had hurt him— uncles who wielded kitchen knives, whatever battles he'd fought in the army that had got him shot, all those shadows that lay heavy on his hard face. One kiss, then another, and she'd felt the coiling tension in him, the heat.

"Your sins are pretty," she'd whispered.

He'd muttered something ferocious in Russian as he'd hauled her mouth to his, then he'd pulled her astride him and surged into her with a dark fury and a deep hunger that had thrilled her all the way through, and she'd been lost in him all over again.

She was still lost.

"For God's sake, Alicia," she bit out, tired of the endless cycle of her own thoughts, and her own appalling weakness. Her voice sounded loud in her small office. "You have work to do."

She had to snap out of this. Her desk was piled high after her two weeks abroad, her in-box was overflowing and she had a towering stack of messages indicating calls she needed to return now that she was back in the country. To say nothing of the report on the Latin American offices she'd visited while away that she had yet to put together, that Charlotte, her supervisor, expected her to present to the team later this week.

But she couldn't sink into her work the way she wanted, the way she usually could. There was that deep current of shame that flared inside of her, bright like some kind of cramp, reminding her of the last night she'd abandoned herself so completely....

At least this time, she remembered every last

second of what she'd done. What *they'd* done. Surely that counted for something.

Her body still prickled now, here, as if electrified, every time she thought of him—and she couldn't seem to stop. Her nipples went hard and between her legs, she ran so hot it almost hurt, and it was such a deep betrayal of who she'd thought she'd become that it made her feel shaky.

Her thighs were still tender from the scrape of his hard jaw. There was a mark on the underside of one breast that he'd left deliberately, reminding her in that harsh, beautiful voice that *wolves bite, solnyshka*, making her laugh and squirm in reckless delight beneath him on that wide, masculine bed where she'd obviously *lost her mind*. Even her hips held memories of what she'd done, reminding her of her overwhelming response to him every now and again with a low, almost-pleasant ache that made her hate herself more every time she felt it.

She'd been hung over before. Ashamed of herself come the dawn. Sometimes that feeling had lingered for days as she'd promised herself that she'd stop partying so hard, knowing deep down that she wouldn't, and hadn't, until that last night in the back garden. But this wasn't *that*. This was worse.

She felt out of control. Knocked flat. Changed, utterly.

A stranger to herself.

Alicia had been so sure the new identity she'd built over these past eight years was a fortress, completely impenetrable, impervious to attack. Hadn't she held Rosie at bay for ages? But one night with Nikolai had showed her that she was nothing but a glass house, precarious and fragile, and a single stone could bring it all crashing down. A single touch.

Not to mention, she hadn't even *thought* about protection that first time. He'd had to *put it in her hand.* Of all her many betrayals of herself that night, she thought that one was by far the most appalling. It made the shame that lived in her that much worse.

The only bright spot in all of this recrimination and regret was that her text to Rosie hadn't gone through. There'd been a big X next to it when she'd looked at her mobile that next morning. And when she'd arrived back at their flat on Sunday morning, Rosie had still been out.

Which meant that no one had any idea what Alicia had done.

"I wish I'd gone home when you did," Rosie had said with a sigh while they sat in their usual Sunday-afternoon café, paging lazily through the Sunday paper and poking at their plates of a traditional full English breakfast. "That place turned *absolutely mental* after hours, and I have to stop getting off with bankers who talk about the flipping property ladder like it's the most thrilling thing on the planet." Then she'd grinned that big grin of hers that meant she didn't regret a single thing, no matter what she said. "Maybe someday I'll actually follow your example."

"What fun would that be?" Alicia had asked lightly, any guilt she'd felt at lying by giant, glaring omission to her best friend drowned out by the sheer relief pouring through her.

Because if Rosie didn't know what she'd done, Alicia could pretend it had never happened.

There would be no discussing Nikolai, that SUV of his or what had happened in it, or that astonishing penthouse that she'd been entirely too gauche not to gape at, openly, when he'd brought her home. There would be no play-by-play description of those things he could do with such ease, that Alicia hadn't known could feel like that. There would certainly be no conversations about all of these confusing and pointless things she felt sloshing around inside of her when she thought about those moments he'd showed her his vulnerable side, as if a man whose last name she didn't know and hadn't asked was something more than a one-night stand.

And if there was no one to talk about it with, all of this urgency, this driving sense of loss, would disappear. *It had to.* Alicia would remain, outwardly, as solid and reliable and predictably boring as she'd become in these past years. An example. The same old Saint Alicia, polishing her halo.

And maybe someday, if she was well-behaved and lucky, she'd believe it again herself.

"Are you ready for the big meeting?"

Her supervisor's dry voice from the open doorway made Alicia jump guiltily in her chair, and it was much harder than it should have been to smile at Charlotte the way she usually did. She was sure what she'd done over her weekend was plastered all over her face. That Charlotte could *see* how filthy she really was, the way her father had. All her sins at a single glance, like that furious creature that bristled on Nikolai's chest.

"Meeting?" she echoed weakly.

"The new celebrity partnership?" Charlotte prompted her. At Alicia's blank look, she laughed. "We all have to show our faces in the conference hall in exactly five minutes, and Daniel delivered a new version of his official presidential lecture on tardiness last week. I wouldn't be late."

"I'll be right along," Alicia promised, and this time, managed a bit of a better smile.

She sighed heavily when Charlotte withdrew, feeling much too fragile. Hollow and raw, as if she was still fighting off that hangover she hadn't had. But she knew it was him. Nikolai. That much fire, that much wild heat, had to have a backlash. She shouldn't be surprised.

This will fade, she told herself, and she should know, shouldn't she? She'd had other things to forget. *It always does, eventually.*

But the current of self-loathing that wound through her then suggested otherwise.

This was not the end of the world. This was no more than a bit of backsliding into shameful behavior, and she wasn't very happy with herself for doing it, but it wouldn't happen again.

No one had walked in on her doing it. No one even knew. Everything was going to be fine.

Alicia blew out a shaky breath, closed down her computer, then made her way toward the big conference hall on the second floor, surprised to find the office already deserted. That could only mean that the celebrity charity in question was a particularly thrilling one. She racked her brain as she climbed the stairs, but she couldn't remember what the last memo had said about it or even if she'd read it.

She hated these meetings, always compulsory and always about standard-waving, a little bit of morale-building, and most of all, PR. They were a waste of her time. Her duties involved the financial planning and off-site management of the charity's regional offices scattered across Latin America. Partnering with much bigger, much more well-known celebrity charities was more of a fundraising and publicity endeavor, which always made Daniel, their president, ecstatic—but didn't do much for Alicia.

She was glad she was a bit late, she thought as

she hurried down the gleaming hallway on the second level. She could slip in, stand at the back, applaud loudly at something to catch Daniel's eye and prove she'd attended, then slip back out again and return to all that work on her messy desk.

Alicia silently eased open the heavy door at the rear of the hall. Down at the front, a man was talking confidently to the quiet, rapt room as she slipped inside.

At first she thought she was imagining it, given where her head had been all day.

And then it hit her. Hard.

She wasn't hearing things.

She knew that voice.

She'd know it anywhere. Her body certainly did.

Rough velvet. Russian. That scratch of whiskey, dark and powerful, commanding and sure.

Nikolai.

Her whole body went numb, nerveless. The door handle slipped from her hand, she jerked her head up to confirm what couldn't possibly be true, couldn't possibly be happening—

The heavy door slammed shut behind her with a terrific crash.

Every single head in the room swiveled toward

her, as if she'd made her entrance in the glare of a bright, hot spotlight and to the tune of a boisterous marching band, complete with clashing cymbals.

But she only saw him.

Him. Nikolai. *Here.*

Once again, everything disappeared. There was only the fearsome blue of his beautiful eyes as they nailed her to the door behind her, slamming into her so hard she didn't know how she withstood it, how she wasn't on her knees from the force of it.

He was even more devastating than she'd let herself remember.

Still dressed all in black, today he wore an understated, elegant suit that made his lethal frame look consummately powerful rather than raw and dangerous, a clever distinction. And one that could only be made by expert tailoring to the tune of thousands upon thousands of pounds. The brutal force of him filled the room, filled her, and her body reacted as if they were still naked, still sprawled across his bed in a tangle of sheets and limbs. She felt too hot, almost feverish. His mouth was a harsh line, but she knew how it tasted and what it could do, and there was something dark and predatory in his eyes that made her tremble deep inside.

And remember. Dear God, what she remembered. What he'd done, how she'd screamed, what he'd promised and how he'd delivered, again and again and again....

It took her much too long to recollect where she was *now*.

Not in a club in Shoreditch this time, filled with drunken idiots who wouldn't recall what they did, much less what she did, but *in her office*. Surrounded by every single person she worked with, all of whom were staring at her.

Nikolai's gaze was so blue. So relentlessly, impossibly, mercilessly blue.

"I'm so sorry to interrupt," Alicia managed to murmur, hoping she sounded appropriately embarrassed and apologetic, the way anyone would after slamming that door—and not as utterly rocked to the core, as lit up with shock and horror, as she felt.

It took a superhuman effort to wrench her gaze away from the man who stood there glaring at her—who wasn't a figment of her overheated imagination, who had the same terrifying power over her from across a crowded room as he'd had in his bed, whom she'd never thought she'd see again, *ever*—and slink to an empty seat in the back row.

She would never know how she did it.

Down in the front of the room, a phalanx of assistants behind him and the screen above him announcing who he was in no uncertain terms, NIKOLAI KOROVIN OF THE KOROVIN FOUNDATION, she saw Nikolai blink. Once.

And then he kept talking as if Alicia hadn't interrupted him. As if he hadn't recognized her—as if Saturday night was no more than the product of her feverish imagination.

As if she didn't exist.

She'd never wished so fervently that she didn't. That she could simply disappear into the ether as if she'd never been, or sink into the hole in the ground she was sure his icy glare had dug beneath her.

What had she been thinking, to touch this man? To give herself to him so completely? Had she been drunk after all? Because today, here and now, he looked like nothing so much as a sharpened blade. Gorgeous and mesmerizing, but terrifying. That dark, ruthless power came off him in waves the way it had in the club, even stronger without the commotion of the music and the crowd, and this time, Alicia understood it.

This was who he was.

She *knew* who he was.

He was Nikolai Korovin. His brother was one of the most famous actors on the planet, which made Nikolai famous by virtue of his surname alone. Alicia knew his name like every other person in her field, thanks to his brilliant, inspired management of the Korovin Foundation since its creation two years ago. People whispered he was a harsh and demanding boss, but always fair, and the amount of money he'd already raised for the good causes the Korovin Foundation supported was staggering.

He was *Nikolai Korovin*, and he'd explored every part of her body with that hard, fascinating mouth. He'd held her in his arms and made her feel impossibly beautiful, and then he'd driven into her so hard, so deep, filling her so perfectly and driving her so out of her mind with pleasure, she had to bear down now to keep from reacting to the memory. He'd made her feel so wild with lust, so deliciously addicted to him, that she'd sobbed the last time she'd shattered into pieces all around him. *She knew how he tasted.* His mouth, his neck, the length of his proud sex. That angry, tattooed monster crouched on his chest. She knew what made him groan, fist his hands into her hair.

More than all of that, she knew how those bright eyes looked when he told her things she had the sense he didn't normally speak of to anyone. She knew too much.

He was Nikolai Korovin, and she didn't have to look over at Daniel's beaming face to understand what it meant that he was here. For Daniel as president, for making this happen. For the charity itself. A partnership with the Korovin Foundation was more than a publicity opportunity—it was a coup. It would take their relatively small charity with global ambitions and slam it straight into the big time, once and for all. And it went without saying that Nikolai Korovin, the legendary CEO of the Korovin Foundation and the person responsible for all its business decisions, needed to be kept happy for that to happen.

That look on his face when he'd seen her had been anything but happy.

Alicia had to force herself to sit still as the implications of this washed through her. She had betrayed herself completely and had a tawdry one-night stand. That was bad enough. But it turned out she'd done it with a man who could end her career.

Eight years ago she'd lost her father's respect and her own self-respect in the blur of a long night she couldn't even recall. Now she could lose her job.

Today. At the end of this meeting. Whenever Nikolai liked.

When you decide to mess up your life, you really go for it, she told herself, fighting back the panic, the prick of tears. *No simple messes for Alicia Teller! Better to go with total devastation!*

Alicia sat through the meeting in agony, expecting something to happen the moment it ended—lightning to strike, the world to come crashing to a halt, Nikolai to summon her to the front of the room and demand her termination at once—but nothing did. Nikolai didn't glance in her direction again. He and his many assistants merely swept from the hall like a sleek black cloud, followed by the still-beaming Daniel and all the rest of the upper level directors and managers.

Alicia told herself she was relieved. This had to be relief, this sharp thing in the pit of her stomach that made it hard to breathe, because nothing else made sense. She'd known he was dangerous the moment she'd met him, not that it had stopped her.

Now she knew exactly *how* dangerous.

She was an idiot. A soon-to-be-sacked idiot.

Her colleagues all grimaced in sympathy as they trooped back downstairs. They thought the fact she'd slammed that door was embarrassing enough. Little did they know.

"Can't imagine having a man like that look at me the way he did you," one said in an undertone. "I think I'd have nightmares!"

"I believe I will," Alicia agreed.

She spent the rest of the afternoon torn between panic and dread. She attacked all the work on her desk, like a drowning woman grasping for something to hold. Every time her phone rang, her heart leaped in her chest. Every time she heard a noise outside her office door, she tensed, thinking she was finished.

Any minute now, she'd be called up to Daniel's

office. She could see it spool out before her like a horror film. Daniel's secretary would message the salacious news to half the office even as Alicia walked to her doom. So not only would Alicia be dismissed from her job because of a tawdry one-night stand with a man most people would have recognized and she certainly should have—but everyone she worked with and respected would know it.

It would be as it had been that morning her father had woken her up and told her what he'd seen, what she'd done—but this time, far more people would know what kind of trollop she was. People she'd impressed with her work ethic over the years would now sit about imagining her naked. *Having sex. With Nikolai.* She felt sick even thinking about it.

"I warned you!" Charlotte said as she stuck her head through the doorway, making Alicia jump again. A quick, terrified glance told her that her supervisor looked...sympathetic. Not horribly embarrassed. Not scandalized in the least. "I told Daniel you were on a call that ran a bit long, so no worries there."

"Thank you." Alicia's voice sounded strained, but Charlotte didn't seem to notice.

"Nikolai Korovin is very intense, isn't he?" Charlotte shook her head. "The man has eyes like a laser beam!"

"I expect he doesn't get interrupted very often," Alicia said, fighting for calm. "I don't think he cares for it."

"Clearly not," Charlotte agreed. And then laughed.

And that was it. No request that Alicia pack up her things or don a scarlet letter. No summons to present herself in Daniel's office to be summarily dismissed for her sexually permissive behavior with the fiercely all-business CEO of their new celebrity partner foundation. Not even the faintest hint of a judgmental look.

But Alicia knew it was coming. She'd not only seen the way Nikolai had looked at her, but now that she knew that he was Nikolai *Korovin,* she was afraid she knew exactly what it meant.

He was utterly ruthless. About everything. The entire internet agreed.

It was only a matter of time until all hell broke loose, so she simply put her head down, kept off the internet because it only served to panic her more, and worked. She stayed long after everyone else had left. She stayed until she'd cleared her desk, because that way, when they tittered behind their hands and talked about how they'd never imagined her acting *that way,* at least they wouldn't be able to say she hadn't done her job.

Small comfort, indeed.

It was almost nine o'clock when she finished, and Alicia was completely drained. She shrugged into her coat and wrapped her scarf around her neck, wishing there was a suit of armor she could put on instead, some way to ward off what she was certain was coming. Dread sat heavy in her stomach, leaden and full, and there was nothing she could do about it but wait to see what Nikolai did. Go home, hole up on the couch with a takeaway and Rosie's usual happy chatter, try to ease this terrible anxiety with bad American television and wait to see what he'd do to her. Because he was Nikolai Korovin, and he could do whatever he liked.

And would. Of that, she had no doubt.

Alicia made her way out of the building, deciding the moment she stepped out into the cold, clear night that she should walk home instead of catching the bus. It was only thirty-five minutes or so at a brisk pace, and it might sort out her head. Tire her out. Maybe even allow her to sleep.

She tucked her hands into her pockets and started off, but had only made it down the front stairs to the pavement when she realized that the big black SUV pulled up to the curb wasn't parked there, but was idling.

A whisper of premonition tingled through her as she drew closer, then turned into a tumult when the back door cracked open before her.

Nikolai Korovin appeared from within the way she should have known he would, tall and thunderous and broadcasting that dark, brooding intensity of his. He didn't have to block her path. He simply closed the door behind him and stood there, taking over the whole neighborhood, darker than the sky above, and Alicia was as unable to move as if he'd pinned her to the ground himself.

She was caught securely in his too-knowing, too-blue gaze all over again, as if he held her in his hands, and the shiver of hungry need that teased down the length of her spine only added insult to injury. She despaired of herself.

If she respected herself at all, Alicia knew with that same old kick of shame in her gut, she wouldn't feel even that tiny little spark of something far too much like satisfaction that he was here. That he'd come for her. As if maybe he was as thrown by what had happened between them as she was...

"Hello, Alicia," Nikolai said, a dark lash in that rough voice of his, velvet and warning and so very Russian, smooth power and all of that danger in every taut line of his beautiful body. He looked fierce. Cold and furious. "Obviously, we need to talk."

CHAPTER FOUR

FOR A MOMENT, Alicia wanted nothing more than to run.

To bolt down the dark street like some desperate animal of prey and hope that this particular predator had better things to do than follow.

Something passed between them then, a shimmer in the dark, and Alicia understood that he knew exactly what she was thinking. That he was picturing the same thing. The chase, the inevitable capture, and *then...*

Nikolai's eyes gleamed dangerously.

Alicia tilted up her chin, settled back on her heels and faced him, calling on every bit of courage and stamina at her disposal. She wasn't going to run. She might have done something she was ashamed of, but she hadn't done it alone. And this time she had to face it—she couldn't skulk off back to university and limit her time back home as she'd done for years until the Reddicks moved to the north.

"Well," she said briskly. "This is awkward."

His cold eyes blazed. He was so different tonight, she thought. A blade of a man gone near incandescent with that icy rage, a far cry from the man she'd thought she'd seen in those quieter moments—the one who had told her things that still lodged in her heart. The change should have terrified her. Instead, perversely, she felt that hunger shiver deeper into her, settling into a hard knot low in her belly, turning into a thick, sweet heat.

"This is not awkward," he replied, his voice deceptively mild. Alicia could see that ferocious look in his eyes, however, and wasn't fooled. "This is a quiet conversation on a deserted street."

"Perhaps the word loses something in translation?" she suggested, perhaps a shade too brightly, as if that was some defense against the chill of him.

"*Awkward,*" he bit out, his accent more pronounced than before and a fascinating pulse of temper in the hinge of his tight jaw, "was looking up in the middle of a business meeting today to see a woman I last laid eyes upon while I was making her come stare right back at me."

Alicia didn't want to think about the last time he'd made her come. She'd thought they were finished after all those long, heated hours. He'd taken that as a challenge. And he'd held her hips between his hands and licked into her with lazy intent, making her writhe against him and sob....

She swallowed, and wished he wasn't watching her. He saw far too much.

"You're looking at me as if I engineered this. I didn't." She eyed him warily, her hands deep in the pockets of her coat and curled into fists, which he couldn't possibly see. Though she had the strangest notion he could. "I thought the point of a one-night stand with no surnames exchanged was that this would never happen."

"Have you had a great many of them, then?"

Alicia pretended that question didn't hit her precisely where she was the most raw, and with a ringing blow.

"If you mean as many as you've had, certainly not." She shrugged when his dark brows rose in a kind of affronted astonishment. "There are no secrets on the internet. Surely you, of all people, must know that. And it's a bit late to tally up our numbers and draw unflattering conclusions, don't you think? The damage is well and truly done."

"That damage," Nikolai said, that rough voice of his too tough, too cold, and that look on his hard face merciless, "is what I'm here to discuss."

Alicia didn't want to lose her job. She didn't want to know what kind of pressure Nikolai was prepared to put on her, what threats he was about to issue. She wanted this to go away again—to be the deep, dark secret that no one ever knew but her.

And it still could be, no matter how pitiless he looked in that moment.

"Why don't we simply blank each other?" she asked, once again a touch too brightly—which she could see didn't fool him at all. If anything, it called attention to her nervousness. "Isn't that the traditional method of handling situations like this?"

He shook his head, his eyes looking smoky in the dark, his mouth a resolute line.

"I do not mix business and pleasure," he said, with a finality that felt like a kick in the stomach. "I do not *mix* at all. The women I sleep with do not infiltrate my life. They appear in carefully orchestrated places of my choosing. They do not ambush me at work. Ever."

Alicia decided that later—much later, when she knew how this ended and could breathe without thinking she might burst into panicked, frustrated tears—she would think about the fact that a man like Nikolai had so many women that he'd developed *policies* to handle them all. *Later.* Right now, she had to fight back, or surrender here and now and lose everything.

"I assure you," she said, as if she had her own set of violated policies and was considering them as she met his gaze, "I feel the same way."

Nikolai shifted, and then suddenly there was no distance between them at all. His hands were on her neck, his thumbs at her jaw, tipping her head back to look up at him. Alicia should have felt attacked, threatened. She should have leaped for safety. Screamed. *Something.*

But instead, everything inside of her went still. And hot.

"I am not here to concern myself with your feelings," he told her in that rough velvet whisper. That fascinating mouth was grim again, but she could almost touch it with hers, if she dared. She didn't. "I am here to eliminate this problem as swiftly and as painlessly as possible."

But his hands were on her. Just as they'd been in the club when he'd told her to run. And she wondered if he was as conflicted as she was, and as deeply. What it would take to see that guarded look on his face again, that vulnerable cast to his beautiful mouth.

"You really are the gift that keeps on giving, Nikolai," she managed to say, retreating to a sarcastic tone, hoping the bite of it might protect her. She even smiled, thinly. "I've never felt happier about my reckless, irresponsible choices."

He let out a short laugh, and whatever expression that was on his hard face then—oddly taut and expectant, dark and hot—was like a flame inside of her. His hands were strong and like brands against her skin. His thumbs moved gently, lazily, as if stroking her jaw of their own accord.

"I don't like sharp women with smart mouths, Alicia," he told her, harsh and low, and every word was a caress against her skin, her sex, as if he was using those long fingers deep in her heat. "I like them sweet. Soft. Yielding and obedient and easily dismissed."

That same electricity crackled between them even here on the cold street, a bright coil that wound tight inside of her, making her feel mad with it. Too close to an explosion she knew she couldn't allow.

"What luck," she said, sharp and smart and nothing like soft at all. "I believe there's a sex shop in the next street, filled with exactly the kind of plastic dolls you prefer. Shall I point you in the right direction?"

He let go of her as if she'd burned him. And she recognized that dark heat in his gaze, the way it changed his expression, the things it did to that mouth.

"Get in the car, Alicia," he ordered her darkly. "I have an aversion to discussing my private life on a public street, deserted or not."

It was her turn to laugh, in disbelief.

"You have to be crazy if you think I'm getting back in that thing," she told him. "I'd rather get down on my hands and knees and crawl across a bed of nails, thank you."

She knew it was a mistake almost before the

words left her mouth, and that sudden wolfish look on his face nearly undid her. It was impossible, then, not to picture herself down on her hands and knees, crawling toward that ravenous heat in his winter eyes she could remember too well, and could see right there before her now.

"I wasn't thinking about sex at present," he said coolly, and even though she could see from that fire in his gaze that he'd imagined much the same thing she had, she felt slapped. Shamed anew. "Why? Were you?"

It was time to go, Alicia realized then. It had been time to go the moment she'd seen that SUV idling at the curb. Before this thing got any worse—and she had no doubt at all that it would.

"It was lovely to finally meet you properly, Mr. Korovin," she said crisply. She put a faint emphasis on the word *properly,* and he blinked, looking almost…abashed? But that was impossible. "I'm sure your partnership with the charity will be a huge boost for us, and I'm as grateful as anyone else. And now I'm going home, where I will continue to actively pretend none of this ever happened. I can only hope you'll do the same."

"You didn't tell me you worked for a children's charity."

She didn't know what she'd expected him to say, but it wasn't that, with that sting of accusation. She eyed him warily. "Neither did you."

"Did you know who I was, Alicia?" Nikolai's face was so hard, his gaze so cold. She felt the chill suddenly, cutting into her. "You stumbled into my arms. Then you stumbled into that conference room today. Convenient." His eyes raked over her, as if looking for evidence that she'd planned this nightmare. "Your next stumble had best not involve any tabloid magazines or tell-all interviews. You won't like how I respond."

But she couldn't believe he truly thought that, she realized when the initial shock of it passed. She'd been in that bed with him. She knew better. Which meant he was lashing out, seeing what would hurt her. *Eliminating problems,* as he'd said he would.

"There's no need to draw out this torture," she told him, proud of how calm she sounded. "If you want me sacked, we both know you can do it easily. Daniel would have the entire staff turn cartwheels down the length of the Mall if he thought

that would please you. Firing me will be a snap."
She squared her shoulders as if she might have
to sustain a blow. As if she already had. "If that's
what you plan to do, I certainly can't stop you."

He stared at her for a long moment. A car raced
past on the street beside them and in the distance
she could hear the rush of traffic on the main
road. Her breath was coming hard and fast, like
she was fighting whole battles in her head while
he only stood there, still and watchful.

"You're a distraction, Alicia," he told her then,
something like regret in his voice. "I can't pretend otherwise."

"Of course you can," she retorted, fighting to
keep calm. "All people do is pretend. I pretended
to be the sort of woman—" She didn't want to
announce exactly what she'd been pretending for
eight years, not to him, so she frowned instead.
"Just ignore me and I'll return the favor. It will
be easy."

"I am not the actor in the family."

"I didn't ask you to play *King Lear,*" she threw
at him, panicked and exasperated in equal measure. "I only asked you to ignore me. How dif-

ficult can that possibly be? A man like you must have that down to a science."

"What an impression you have of me," Nikolai said after a moment, his voice silken, his eyes narrow. "I treated you very well, Alicia. Have you forgot so soon? You wept out your gratitude, when you weren't screaming my name."

She didn't need the reminder. She didn't need the heat of it, the wild pulse in her chest, between her legs.

"I was referring to your wealth and status," Alicia said, very distinctly. "Your position. The fact you have armies of assistants to make sure no one can approach you without your permission. Not your…"

"Particular talents?" His voice was mild enough as he finished the thought for her. The effect his words had on her, inside her, was not.

But then he leaned back against the side of his car, as if he was perfectly relaxed. Even his face changed, and she went still again, because there was something far more predatory about him in this moment than there had been before. It scraped the air thin.

"I have a better solution," he said, in the confident and commanding tone she recognized from the conference room. "I don't need to fire you, necessarily. It will serve my purposes far better to use this situation to my advantage."

Alicia could only shake her head, looking for clues on that face of his that gave nothing away. "I don't know what that means."

"It means, Alicia," he said almost softly, a wolf's dangerous smile in those winter eyes if not on that hard mouth, "that I need a date."

He could use this, Nikolai thought, while Alicia stared up at him as if he'd said that last sentence in Russian instead of English. He could use her.

A problem well managed could become a tool. And every tool could be a weapon, in the right hands. Why not Alicia?

He'd expected her to want more than Saturday night—they always did. And the sex they'd had had been…troubling. He'd known it while it was happening. He'd known it in between, when he'd found himself talking of things he never, ever talked about. He'd known it when he'd opened his eyes to watch her tiptoe from his room on Sunday morning, and had discovered he wanted her to stay.

He knew it now, remembering her sweet, hot mouth against his tattoo as if she'd blessed that snarling representation of the monster in him. As if she'd made it sacred, somehow. The moment he'd seen her, he'd expected she would try to leverage that, take it from him somehow. He'd planned to make it clear to her she had to go—before she could try.

But she claimed she wanted to ignore him. He should have been thrilled.

He told himself he was.

"I'm sorry." Her voice was carefully blank when she finally spoke, to match the expression on her face. "Did you say you needed a *date?*"

"I did." It occurred to him that he was enjoying himself, for the first time since he'd looked up and seen her standing in that conference room, in clear violation of all his rules. "There is a Christmas ball in Prague that I must attend in a few weeks, and it will go much more smoothly with a woman on my arm."

These things were always better with a date, it was true. It didn't matter who it was. The presence of any date at his side would repel most of the vulturelike women who always circled him like he was fresh meat laid out in the hot sun, allowing Nikolai to concentrate on business. And in the case of this particular charity ball, on Veronika—who had only this morning confirmed that she and her lover would attend.

Because Nikolai had realized, as he looked at her in the light of the streetlamps and thought strategy instead of containment, that Alicia could very well turn out to be the best weapon yet in his dirty little war.

"I'm certain there are hordes of women who would love nothing more than to fill that opening for you," she said, with none of the deference or courtesy he was used to from his subordinates and dates alike. There was no reason on earth he should find that intriguing. "Perhaps one of your many assistants has a sign-up sheet? A call list? Maybe even an audition process to weed out the lucky winner from the multitudes?"

He'd told her he liked sweet and biddable, and he did. But he liked this, too. He liked the way she talked to him, as if it hadn't occurred to her that she should fear him like everyone else did.

It made him want to lick her until all of that tartness melted all over him, and he didn't want to examine that particular urge any closer.

"Something like that," he said. "But it's all very tedious. All I want is a pretty dress, a polite smile. I don't have time for the games."

"Or the person, apparently," she said, her voice dry. "I'm sure that's very rewarding for whichever pretty dress you choose. But what does this have to do with me?"

Nikolai smiled, adrenaline moving through him the way it always did before a tactical strike. Before another win.

"You want nothing to do with me." His voice was a silken threat in the cold night. "Or so you claim."

"You're right," she said, but her voice caught. "I don't."

"Then it's perfect," he said. "It's only a handful of weeks until the ball. We'll allow ourselves to be photographed on a few dates. The world will think I'm smitten, as I am very rarely seen with the same woman more than once. More specifically, my ex-wife will think the same. And as she has always greatly enjoyed her fantasy that she is the only woman to have any power over me, and has never been one to resist a confrontation, it will put her right where I want her."

She stared at him. "And where is that, exactly?"

"Veronika and I need to have a conversation," Nikolai said with cool dismissal. "Hopefully, our last. The idea that I might have moved on will expedite that, I think."

"How tempting," she said after a moment, her voice as arid as that look in her eyes. "I've always aspired to be cold-bloodedly used to make another woman jealous, of course. It's truly every girl's dream. But I think I'll pass."

"This has nothing to do with jealousy," he said impatiently. "The only thing left between Veronika and me is spite. If that. I'm sure you'll see it yourself at the ball."

"Even more appealing. But still—no."

"Your whole office saw me stare at you today." He shrugged when her eyes narrowed. "They could hardly miss it. How much of a leap will it be for them to imagine that was the beginning of an infatuation?"

"But they won't have to make that leap." Her

eyes were glittering again. "I've declined your lovely offer and we're going to ignore each other."

"I don't think so." He watched her take that in. Knew she didn't like it. Found he didn't much care if she was happy about it, so long as she did it. "I'm going to take an interest in you, Alicia. Didn't you know? Everybody loves a romance."

"They won't believe it." Her voice sounded thick, as if the idea of it horrified her, and he was perverse enough to take that as a challenge. "They won't believe someone like you could get infatuated at all, much less with me."

He smiled. "They will. And more to the point, so will Veronika."

And he could kill two birds with one stone. He could dig into this attraction, the unacceptable intoxication this woman made him feel, and in so doing, strip away its power over him. Make certain he never again felt the need to unburden himself in such a shockingly uncharacteristic manner to a total stranger. At the same time, he could use Veronika's smug certainty about her place in his life against her. It was perfect.

Alicia stared back at him, so hard he thought he could hear her mind racing.

"Why bring any of this into the office at all?" she asked, sounding frustrated. Panicked, even. "If you want me to go to this ball, fine. I'll do it, but I don't see why anyone needs to know about it but us. No unlikely romance necessary."

"And how will that work?" he asked mildly. "When pictures of us at that ball show up in all the papers, and they will, it will look as if we were keeping our relationship a secret. As if we were hiding something. Think of the gossip then."

"You said you're not an actor," she said. "Yet this seems like a very elaborate bit of theater."

"I told you, you're a distraction," he replied, almost gently. He wanted to show her what he meant. To bury his face in that crook of her neck. To make her quiver for him the way he knew he could. Only the fact he wanted it too much kept him from it. "I don't allow distractions, Alicia. I neutralize them or I use them for my own ends."

"I don't want to be in any papers." Her voice was low, her eyes intense on his. It took him a moment to realize she was panicked. A better man might not have enjoyed that. "I don't want *pictures* of me out there, and certainly not with you."

"There's a certain liberty in having no choices,

Alicia," he told her, not sure why it bothered him that she was so opposed to a picture *with him*. It made his voice harsher. "It makes life very simple. Do what I tell you to do, or look for a new job."

Nikolai didn't think that was the first moment it had occurred to her that he held all the power here, but it was no doubt when she realized he had every intention of using it as he pleased. He saw it on her face. In her remarkable eyes.

And he couldn't help but touch her again then, sliding his hand over her cheek as he'd done before. He felt the sweet heat of her where his fingertips touched her hairline, the chill of her soft skin beneath his palm. And that wild heat that was only theirs, sparking wild, charging through him.

Making him almost wish he was a different man.

She wore a thick black coat against the cold, a bright red scarf looped around her elegant neck. Her ink-black curls were pulled back from her face with a scrap of brightly patterned fabric, and he knew that beneath it she was dressed in even more colors, bright colors. Emerald greens and chocolate browns. She was so bright it made his head spin, even here in the dark. It made him achingly hard.

She is nothing more than an instrument, he told himself. *Another weapon for your arsenal. And soon enough, this intoxication will fade into nothing.*

"Please," she whispered, and he wished he were the kind of man who could care. Who could soothe her. But he wasn't, no matter what he told her in the dark. "You don't understand. I don't want to lose my job, but I can't do this."

"You can," Nikolai told her. "And you will." He felt more in control than he had since she'd slammed into him at the edge of that dance floor, and he refused to give that up again. He wouldn't. "I'll be the one infatuated, Alicia. You need only surrender."

She shook her head, but she didn't pull her face from his grasp, and he knew what that meant even if she didn't. He knew what surrender looked like, and he smiled.

"Feel free to refuse me at first," he told Alicia then, his voice the only soft thing about him, as if he was a sweet and gentle lover and these words were the poetry he'd told her he didn't write. As if he was someone else. Maybe it would help her to think so. "Resist me, if you can. That will only make it look better."

"I won't do it," Alicia told him, hearing how unsteady her voice was and hating that he heard it, too. Hating all of this. "I won't play along."

"You will," he said in that implacable way that made something inside her turn over and shiver, while that half smile played with the corner of his hard mouth as if he knew something she didn't. "Or I'll have you sacked so fast it will make your head spin. And don't mistake sexual attraction for mercy, Alicia. I don't have any."

"Of course not," she bit out, as afraid that she would burst into tears right there as she was that she would nestle further into his hand, both impulses terrible and overwhelming at once. "You're the big, bad wolf. Fangs and teeth. I get the picture. I still won't do it."

She wrenched herself away from the terrible beguilement of his touch then, and ran down the street the way she should have at the start, panic biting at her heels as if she thought he might chase her.

He didn't—but then, he didn't have to chase her personally. His words did that for him. They haunted her as she tossed and turned in her sleepless bed that night. They moved over her like an itch she couldn't scratch. Like a lash against her skin, leaving the kind of scars he wore in their wake. Kitchen knives and bullets.

Do what I tell you to do.

Alicia was appalled at herself. He could say terrible things, propose to use her in some sick battle with his ex-wife, and still, she wanted him. He was mean and surly and perfectly happy to threaten her—and she wanted him. She lay awake in her bed and shivered when she thought about that last, simple touch, his hand hot despite the chill of the night air, holding her face so gently, making everything inside her run together and turn into honey.

Because that fool inside of her wanted that touch to mean something more. Wanted this attraction between them to have more to do with that vulnerability he'd shown her than the sex they'd had.

Wanted Saturday night to be different from that terrible night eight years ago.

He wants to use you, nothing more, she reminded herself for the millionth time, punching at her pillow in exhausted despair. *It means nothing more than that.*

But Alicia couldn't have pictures of herself in the tabloids. Not at all, and certainly not in the company of a man who might have been called a playboy, had he been less formidable. Not that it mattered what they called him—her father would know exactly what he was. Too wealthy, too hard. Too obvious. A man like that wanted women for one thing only, and her father would know it.

He would think she was back to old tricks. She knew he would.

Alicia shuddered, her face pressed into her pillow. She could *see* that awful look on her father's face that hideous morning as if he stood in front of her the way he'd done then.

"He is a *married man*. You know his wife, his children," her father had whispered, looking as deeply horrified as Alicia had felt.

"Dad," she'd managed to say, though her head had pounded and her mouth had been like sand. "Dad, I don't know what happened…. It's all—I don't remember—"

"I know what happened," he'd retorted, disgust

plain in his voice and all across his face. "I saw you, spread-eagled on the grass with a *married man,* our *neighbor—*"

"Dad—" she'd tried again, tears in her voice and her eyes, afraid she might be sick.

"The way you dress, the way you flaunt yourself." He'd shaken his head, condemnation and that deep disgust written all over him. "I knew you dressed like a common whore, Alicia, but I never thought you'd *act* like one."

She couldn't go through that again, she thought then, staring in mute despair at her ceiling. She wouldn't go through it again, no matter how *infatuated* Nikolai pretended he was. No matter what.

He was going to have to fire her, she decided. She would call his bluff.

"No," she said, very firmly, when a coworker ran up to her the following day as she fixed herself a midmorning cup of tea and breathlessly asked if she'd *heard.* "Heard what?"

But she had a terrible suspicion she could guess. Ruthless and efficient, that was Nikolai.

"Nikolai Korovin *expressly* asked after you at the meeting this morning!" the excitable Melanie from the PR team whispered in that way of hers that alerted the entire office and most of the surrounding neighborhood, her eyes wide and pale cheeks red with the thrill of it all. "He *grilled* the team about you! Do you think that means he…?"

She couldn't finish that sentence, Alicia noted darkly. It was too much for Melanie. The very idea of Nikolai Korovin's interest—his *infatuation*—made the girl practically crumple into a shivering heap at Alicia's feet.

"I imagine he's the kind of man who keeps an annotated enemies list within arm's reach and several elaborate revenge plots at the ready," Alicia said as calmly as possible, dumping as much cold water on this fire of his as she could, even though she suspected it wouldn't do any good. "He certainly doesn't *like* me, Melanie."

The other woman didn't looked particularly convinced, no doubt because Alicia's explanation flew in the face of the grand romance she'd already concocted in her head. Just as Nikolai had predicted.

"No, thank you," Alicia told the emissary from his army of assistants two days after that, who walked up to Alicia as she stood in the open plan part of the office with every eye trained on her and asked if she might want to join them all for a meal after work?

"Mr. Korovin wanted me to tell you that it's a restaurant in Soho he thinks you'd quite enjoy," the woman persisted, her smile never dropping from her lips. "One of his favorites in London. And his treat, of course."

Alicia's heart hammered in her chest so hard she wondered for a panicked moment if she was having some kind of heart attack. Then she remembered how many people were watching her, much too avidly, and forced a polite smile in return.

"I'm still catching up from my trip," she lied. "I'll have to work late again, I'm afraid. But please do thank Mr. Korovin for thinking of me."

Somehow, that last part didn't choke her.

By the end of that week, the fact that ruthless and somewhat terrifying billionaire Nikolai Korovin had *taken an interest* in Alicia was the only thing anyone in the office seemed able to talk about, and he'd accomplished it without lowering himself to speak to her directly. She felt hunted, trapped, and she hadn't even seen him since that night on the street.

He was diabolical.

"I believe Nikolai Korovin wants to *date* you, Alicia," Charlotte said as they sat in her office on Friday morning, going over the presentation for their team meeting later that afternoon. She grinned widely when Alicia looked at her. "I don't know whether to be excited or a bit overwhelmed at the idea of someone like him dating a normal person."

"This is so embarrassing," Alicia said weakly, which was perhaps the first honest thing she'd said on the topic all week. "I honestly don't know why he's doing this."

"Love works in mysterious ways," Charlotte singsonged, making Alicia groan.

Everybody loves a romance, he'd said in that cold, cynical voice of his. Damn him.

"This is a man who could date anyone in the world, and has done," Alicia said, trying to sound lighter, breezier, than she felt. "Why on earth should a man like that want to date *me?*"

"You didn't drop at his feet on command, obviously," Charlotte said with a shrug. Only because he hadn't issued that particular command that night, Alicia thought sourly, fighting to keep her expression neutral. "Men like Nikolai Korovin are used to having anything they desire the moment they desire it. Ergo, they desire most what they can't have."

Alicia hadn't been so happy to see the end of a work week in years. She hated him, she told herself that weekend, again and again and again, until she could almost pretend that she really did. That it was that simple.

"I hate him," she told Rosie, taking out her feelings on the sad little boil-in-the-bag chicken curry they'd made for Sunday dinner with a violent jab of her fork. It had been two blessed Nikolai-free days. She couldn't bear the thought of what tomorrow might bring. "He's incredibly unprofessional. He's made the whole office into a circus! Nothing but gossip about him and me, all day every day!"

Rosie eyed Alicia from her side of the sofa, her knees pulled up beneath her and her blond hair piled haphazardly on her head.

"Maybe he likes you."

"No. He does not. This is some kind of sick game he's playing for his own amusement. That's the kind of man he is."

"No kind of man goes to all that trouble," her

friend said slowly. "Not for a game. He really could simply like you, Alicia. In his own terrifyingly wealthy sort of way, I mean."

"He doesn't like *me,* Rosie," Alicia retorted, with too much heat, but she couldn't stop it. "The women he likes come with their own *Vogue* covers."

But she could see that Rosie was conjuring up Cinderella stories in her head, like everyone else, as Nikolai had known they would. Alicia felt so furious, so desperate and so trapped, that she shook with it. She felt his manipulation like a touch, like he was sitting right there next to her, that big body of his deceptively lazy, running his amused fingers up and down her spine.

You wish you were anything as uncomplicated as furious, a little voice taunted her, deep inside.

"Maybe you should play along," Rosie said then, and she grinned wide. "It's not going to be a drink down at the pub on a date with the likes of him, is it? He's the sort who has *mistresses,* not *girlfriends.* He could fly you to Paris for dinner. He could whisk you off to some private island. Or one of those great hulking yachts they always have."

"He could ruin my reputation," Alicia countered, and yet despite herself, wondered what being Nikolai's *mistress* would entail—what sort of lover he would be, what kind of sensual demands he would make if he had more than one night to make them. All of that lethal heat and all the time in the world… How could anyone survive it? She shoved the treacherous thoughts aside. "He could make things very difficult for me at work."

"Only because they'll all be seething with jealousy," Rosie said with a dismissive sniff. "And your reputation could use a little ruining."

Because she couldn't imagine what it was like to *actually* be ruined, Alicia knew. To have gone and ruined herself so carelessly, so irrevocably. She couldn't know what it was like to see that disgust in her own father's eyes whenever he looked at her. To feel it in her own gut, like a cancer.

Rosie smiled again, wickedly. "And I think Nikolai Korovin sounds like the kind of man who knows his way around a ruining."

Alicia only stabbed her chicken again. Harder. And then scowled at the television as if she saw anything at all but Nikolai, wherever she looked.

CHAPTER FIVE

ALICIA WAS RUNNING a file up to Charlotte's office the following week when she finally ran into him, larger than life, sauntering down the stairs in the otherwise-empty stairwell as if he hadn't a care in the world.

The shock of it—the force and clamor that was Nikolai—hit her as hard as it had at the club. As it had outside the office building that night. Making her feel restless in her own skin. Electric.

Furious, she told herself sternly.

He saw her instantly and smiled, that tug in the corner of his hard mouth that made her insides turn to water no matter how much she wished it didn't. No matter how much she wanted to be immune to it. To him.

Because whatever she was, whatever this *thing* was that made her so aware of him, she certainly wasn't immune.

And Nikolai knew it.

He moved like water, smooth and inexorable. He seemed bigger than he actually was, as if he was so powerful he couldn't be contained and so expanded to fit—and to effortlessly dominate—any and all available space. Even an ordinary stairwell. Today he wore another absurdly well-fitting suit in his usual black, this one a rapturous love letter to his lean, muscled, dangerous form. He looked sinfully handsome, ruthless and cool, wealthy beyond imagining, and it infuriated her. So deeply it hurt.

Alicia told herself that was all it did.

"This is harassment," she informed him as she marched up the stairs, her heels clicking hard against each step, her tone as brisk as her spine was straight.

"No," he said, his gaze on hers. "It isn't."

Alicia stopped moving only when she'd reached the step above him, enjoying the fact it put her on eye level with him, for once. Even if those eyes were far too blue, bright and laughing at her, that winter cold moving in her, heating her from within.

She hated him.

God, how she wished she could hate him.

"It most certainly is," she corrected him with a bit of his own frostiness. "And I hate to break this to you when you've gone ahead and made your pretend infatuation so public, but it's actually quite easy to resist you."

"Is it?" He shouldn't sound so amused. So indulgent.

She would have scowled at him, but thought he would read that as weakness. Instead, she tilted up her chin and tried to project the kind of tough, cool competence she wished she felt as she called his bluff to his face.

"I'm not going to take part in your little bit of revenge theater no matter how much time you spend feeding the office gossip mill," she told him. Tough. Calm. Cool. "If you want to have me fired because you took me home from a club of your own free will, go right ahead." She let that sit there for a moment, then angled her head ever so slightly closer to his, for emphasis. "I didn't do anything wrong, I'm not afraid of you and I'd advise you try to communicate with your ex-wife through more traditional channels."

Nikolai simply…shifted position.

He moved with a primal grace that robbed her of

speech, pivoting without seeming to do so much as breathe. All Alicia knew was that she was facing him one moment and the next her back was up against the wall. As if he'd *willed* her to let him cage her there, his hands flat against the smooth wall on either side of her face.

He hadn't laid so much as a single finger upon her. He didn't now. He leaned in.

Much too close, and her body reacted as if he'd plugged her into the nearest socket. The white-hot light of this shocking heat between them pulsed through her, making her gasp. Her body betrayed her in a shivering flush, sensation scraping through her, making her skin pull taut, her breasts feel suddenly full and that wet, hot hunger punch its way into her belly before settling down between her legs. Where it stayed, a wild and greedy need, and all of it his. *His.*

As if she was, too.

"What the hell are you doing?" But it was no more than a whisper, and it gave her away as surely as that treacherous ache inside of her that Alicia was sure he could sense, somehow.

"I am a man possessed," Nikolai murmured, his mouth so close to hers she felt the pull of it, the ache, roll through her like a flash of pain, despite the hint of laughter she could hear in his voice. "Infatuated. Just as I promised you."

"I can see why your brother is the famous actor while you storm about, growling at other rich men and demanding their money." But her voice was little more than a breath, completely insubstantial, and she had to dig her fingers into the folder she carried to keep from touching that glorious chest that was right there in front of her, taunting her. "Because you're not terribly convincing, and by the way, I'm fairly certain this counts as stalking."

"Those are very strong words, Alicia." He didn't sound concerned. Nikolai rested his considerable, sleek weight on his hands and surrounded her. Hemmed her in. Let his body remind her of all those things she wanted to forget. *Needed* to forget. "Harassment. Stalking."

"Strong, yes." She could feel her pulse in her throat, a frantic staccato. "And also accurate."

Alicia felt more than heard his small laugh against the tender skin of her neck, and she knew he saw the goose bumps that prickled there when he lifted that knowing gaze to hers.

"This is the first time I've seen you inside this

office since you walked into the conference hall."
Nikolai didn't move back. He gave her no room to
breathe. If she tried to twist away, to escape him
the way she wanted to do, she would have to brush
up against him—and she didn't dare do that. She
couldn't trust herself. Not when he smelled like
winter. Not when she had the alarming urge to
bury her face in his chest. "I haven't followed you
around making suggestive comments. I extended
a single invitation to you, Alicia. I didn't even do
it myself. And you declined it without any reper-
cussions at all."

"Says the man who has me pinned up against
a wall."

"I'm not touching you," Nikolai pointed out,
that dangerously lazy gleam in his bright gaze.
"I'm not restraining you in any way. I could, of
course." That gleam grew hotter, making her toes
curl inside her shoes, making that need inside her
rage into a wildfire. Making her despair of herself. "All you have to do is ask."

"I want you to stop this," she managed to get
out, desperate to fight off the maelstrom he'd un-
leashed in her, the images carnal and tempting

that chased through her head and made her much too aware of how weak she was.

How perilously close to compounding the error she'd already made with this man, right here in her office. In the *stairwell*. Every inch of her the whore her father had called her.

"Which *this?*" He sounded impossibly male, then. Insufferably smug, as if he knew exactly how close she was to capitulation. "Be specific."

She shifted then, and it was agonizing. He was *right there,* and she knew she couldn't allow herself to touch him, not even by accident—but she was terribly afraid she wasn't going to be able to help herself. How could she fight herself *and* him?

"I'd rather be sacked right now than have to put up with this," she whispered fiercely.

He laughed again then, and she wished that sound didn't get to her. She wished she could simply ignore it and him along with it. But it made him that much more beautiful, like a perfect sunset over a rugged mountain, and it made something inside of her ignite no matter how much she wished it didn't.

"You and I both know I could prove you a liar." He dropped his head slightly, and inhaled, as if pulling the scent of her skin deep into his lungs, and that fire in her began to pulse, greedy and insistent. Her nipples pressed against the soft fabric of her dress, and she was terrified he'd see it. Terrified he'd *know.* "How long do you think it would take, *solnyshka?* One second? Two? How long before you wrap yourself around me and beg?"

Of course he knew. Hadn't that long night with him taught her anything?

Alicia stiffened, panic like a drumbeat inside of her, but it only seemed to make that fire in her burn hotter. Nikolai moved even closer, somehow, though that shouldn't have been possible, and he was so big, so powerful, that it was as if nothing existed except the breadth of his shoulders. He surrounded her, and there was a part of her way down deep that wasn't at all conflicted. That simply exulted in it. In him.

But that was the part that had started all this. The part that had looked up into his face in that dark club and surrendered, there and then. She couldn't succumb to his version of dark magic again. She had too much to lose.

"You don't understand," she said hurriedly, almost desperately. "This is—you are—" She pulled in a breath. "I'm afraid—"

But she couldn't tell Nikolai Korovin the things she feared. She couldn't say them out loud, and anyway, this was only a bitter little game to him. The ways she hated herself, the ways she'd let herself down, the way she'd destroyed her relationship with her father—he didn't need to know about any of that.

She couldn't understand why she had the strange urge to tell him anyway, when she'd never told a soul.

It seemed to take him a very long time to pull his head back far enough to look her in the eyes, to study her too-hot face. Even through her agitation, she could see him grow somber as he watched her. Darker. He pushed back from the wall, letting his hands drop to his sides, and Alicia told herself that was exactly what she'd wanted.

"Good," he said quietly, an expression she couldn't read on his hard face. "You should be afraid of me. You should have been afraid that night."

She scowled at him, not caring anymore what he read into it.

"For God's sake," she snapped, not liking that look on his face and not at all sure why it bothered her so much and so deeply. "I'm not afraid of *you*."

That sat there between them, telling him things she should have kept to herself, and the expression on his face made her think of that moment in his bed, suddenly. When he'd talked of kitchen knives and sins and she'd kissed his tattoo, as if she could kiss it all away. As if he was wounded.

"I thought you liked the fact that I *don't* want you," she said after a moment, when all he did was stare at her, in a manner she might have called haunted if it was someone other than Nikolai. "Why are you so determined to prove otherwise?"

"You mistake me." His voice was silky then, but there was a dark kick beneath it, and it shivered over her skin like a caress. "I know you want me. I still want you. I told you this was a distraction." He stuck his hands in his pockets, shifting back on his heels, and his expression grew cooler. More distant. Assessing her. "It's your disinterest in having any kind of connection to me, your horror at the very idea, that makes the rest of this possible."

"And by that do you mean keeping my job?" she asked, ignoring his talk of who wanted who, because she didn't dare let herself think about it. She couldn't go there, or who knew what would become of her? "Or the twisted game you feel you need to play with your ex-wife?"

Nikolai only stared back at her, his face a study in ice. Impassive and cool.

"Let me guess," she said tightly. "You only want what you can't have."

"But you don't qualify, Alicia," he said, in that dangerously soft way of his that was like a seismic event inside of her, and she had to fight to hide the aftershocks. "I've already had you."

"That was a mistake," she retorted, and she wanted to play it down. Laugh, smile. But his eyes flashed and she knew she'd sounded too dark. Too close to *hurt*. "There won't be a repeat."

"You don't want to challenge me to prove you wrong." His winter eyes probed hers, moved over her face, saw things she didn't want to share. "Or perhaps you do."

That last was a low growl. Wolf again, not man, and she wasn't sure she could survive it without imploding. Without betraying herself all over again, and there was no *wild night* to lose herself in, not here in this chilly stairwell. No pounding music, no shouting crowd. She felt the danger in him, the profound sensual threat, like heat all around her, seducing her without a single word or touch. She could smell that scent that was only his, the faint smoke and crisp slap of winter. She felt the strength of him, that lethal power, and her fingers ached to explore it again, every last lean muscle, until he groaned beneath her hands.

And she *wanted*.

Suddenly, and with every last cell in her body, Alicia wanted to be someone else. Someone free of her past, free to throw herself heedlessly into all of this wondrous fire and not care if it swallowed her whole. Someone who could do what she liked with this man without bringing her whole world down around her all over again.

Someone very much like the person she'd seemed to think she was the night she'd met him.

But she couldn't. And Nikolai still didn't touch her, which almost made it worse.

"It's time to move into the public phase of this arrangement," he told her in that distant way again, as if this was a planned meeting in the stairwell to calmly discuss the calendar of events that would lead to her downfall. "We'll start with dinner tomorrow night. There are things we need to discuss."

"What a lovely invitation—"

"It's not a request."

She studied him for a moment, all that ice and steel. "I'm otherwise engaged."

"Cancel."

"And if I refuse?"

Nikolai's smile turned dangerous. Her stomach contracted hard at the sight, and the ache of it sank low, turning molten and making her despair of herself anew.

It was that easy. *She* was that easy.

"You can try to run from me if you like." He looked intrigued at the prospect, and something dark and sensual twisted through her, leaving marks. "But I should give you fair warning—I'll find you. And you might not like the mood I'm in when I do."

"Fine," she made herself say, because she couldn't think of an alternate plan, certainly not while he stood there in front of her with a look on his face that told her he'd love to spend more time convincing her. She couldn't have that. And she certainly didn't want him to pursue her through the streets of London, to run her to ground like some mutinous fox, which she had no doubt he would do…. Did she? "Tomorrow night we'll suffer through the date from hell. That sounds delightful. Where do you want me to meet you?"

He reached out then and she braced herself, but he only wrapped a sprig of her curls around his finger, gave them a tug that was very nearly gentle, then let his hand drop, an odd cast to his fierce, proud mouth as he did it.

There was no reason at all that should pierce her heart.

"Don't try to top from the bottom, Alicia," he said, laughter in his brilliant gaze for a moment before it chilled into something much harder. More ruthless. "I'll let you know what I want tomorrow. And you'll do it. Because I really will have you fired if you don't, and despite this entertaining display of bravado, I think you know it."

And there it was.

She didn't want to lose her job—which meant she'd have to figure out how to survive losing her father all over again, once there were pictures to prove once more that she was nothing but a whore. And if there was a tiny spark inside of her, because some foolish part of her wished this wasn't all a game, that it wasn't all for show, that she was the kind of person men didn't use, she did her best to ignore it.

"I don't want to do this." Her voice was small, but still firm, and she thought she'd be proud, later, that she kept her head high. Even in defeat. "Any of it."

"I know you don't," Nikolai said, whole winters in his voice, in his beautiful eyes, so blue she wanted to cry. And there was a flash of something there, bright for a moment and then gone, as if this was more of a struggle for him than it seemed. It scared her, how much she wanted to believe that. "But you will."

Alicia sat where Nikolai had put her, at the corner of the dark wood table that stretched across a significant length of the great two-story room that was the center of his apartment, all low-slung modern couches and soaring windows. Nikolai could read her stiff tension in the way she sat, the way she held her lips too tight, the precise, angry movements of her hands.

His staff had served a five-star dinner that she'd barely touched. Nikolai hadn't spoken a word, and she hadn't broken the silence. Now she was pushing her dessert around on her plate, and he was well aware that her agitation level had skyrocketed even higher than before.

Bastard that he was, that amused him. He lounged in his seat, at the head of the table with her at his right, and studied her. He would figure her out. He would solve the mystery of this woman and when he did, lose interest in her. It was inevitable.

But he hadn't anticipated he would enjoy the process quite this much.

"You're a terrible date," he told her, and her dark eyes flashed when they met his. Then, after a moment, she rolled them. *At* him.

No one else would dare.

"Thank you," she said in that dry way that made him want her beneath him, right there on the table. He had to yank himself back under control, and it was significantly harder than it should have been.

Focus, he ordered himself. "I can see why you're considered such a catch."

"This is an excellent opportunity to discuss my expectations," Nikolai said, as if her fearless defiance didn't make him want to lick his way into the heat of her, to make her writhe and sob in his hands. And he would, he promised himself, as soon as they came to an understanding. "Dating me comes with a number of requirements, Alicia. Making appropriate dinner conversation is only one of them."

"You're perfectly capable of making conversation," she pointed out in the same dry tone. "In fact, you're doing it right now, though I don't know if it qualifies as 'appropriate.'" She considered him for a moment, a small smile that he didn't like, yet found he wanted to taste, flirting with her full lips. "I suspected there must be some kind of application process and I'm delighted I'm right, but I'm not dating you. This isn't real." Her gaze turned hard on his. "This is blackmail."

"Call it whatever you like," he said, with a careless shrug. "The result is the same."

"Blackmail," she repeated, very distinctly. "I think you'll find that's what it's called when you force someone into doing something they don't want to do by holding something else over their head."

Nikolai could see all of that temper in her dark gaze, the flash of it when she couldn't hide her feelings. She wore a sleeveless wool top tonight in a deep aubergine shade, with a neck that drooped down low and left her smooth, toned arms on display, looking soft and sweet in the candlelight. But most important, he could see every time she tensed, every time she forced herself to relax, written up and down the lean, elegant shape of those arms and all across her slender frame. Like now, when she forced her shoulders back and down, then smiled at him as if she wasn't agitated at all.

She didn't know, yet, that he could read her body the way others read words on a page. But she would learn, and he would greatly enjoy teaching her. First, though, they had business to take care of. If it alarmed him that he had to remind himself of business before pleasure for the first time in living memory, he ignored it.

"There is a confidentiality agreement that you'll need to sign," he told her, dismissing her talk of blackmail, which he could see she didn't like.

"Beyond that, I have only standard expectations. Don't venture out into public unless you're prepared to be photographed, as terrible pictures of you could lead to negative coverage of me, which is unacceptable. I'll let you know what pleases me—"

"If you mention a single thing about altering my appearance to suit your tastes, whatever those might be," she said almost conversationally, though there was murder in her eyes, "I will stab you with this fork. I'm not dating you, Nikolai. I'm acquiescing to your bizarre demands because I want to keep my job, but we're not reenacting some sick little version *My Fair Lady*. I don't care about pleasing you."

Nikolai was definitely enjoying himself. Especially when he saw that little shiver move through her, and knew they were both thinking about all the ways she could please him. All the ways she had. He smiled slightly.

"Is that a passive-aggressive demand that I compliment your looks?" he asked silkily. "I had no idea you were so insecure, Alicia. I'd have thought the fact that I had my mouth on every inch of that gorgeous body of yours would have told you my feelings on that topic in no uncertain terms. Though I'm happy to repeat myself."

"I may stab you with this fork anyway." She met his gaze then and smiled. But he could see that her breathing had quickened. He knew arousal when he saw it. When he'd already tasted it. All of that heat and need, sweet against her dark skin. "Fair warning."

"You can always try."

She considered that for a moment, then sat back against her chair, inclining her head slightly as if she held the power here and was granting him permission to carry on.

"Don't ever keep me waiting," Nikolai said, continuing as if she hadn't interrupted him. "Anywhere. For any reason. My time is more valuable than yours."

Her eyes narrowed at that, but she didn't speak. Perhaps she was learning, he thought—but he hoped not. He really hoped not. He wanted her conquered, not coerced. He wanted to do it himself, step by delectable step.

"Don't challenge my authority. In your case, I'll allow some leeway because I find that smart mouth of yours amusing, but only a little leeway,

Alicia, and never in public. Your role is as an ornament. I won't tolerate disrespect or disobedience. And I will tell you what you are to me, explicitly—never imagine yourself anything else. I can't stress that enough."

The silence between them then felt tighter. Hotter. Breathless, as if the great room had shrunk down until there was nothing but the two of them and the gently flickering candles. And her eyes were big and dark and he realized he could no longer read the way she looked at him.

"You're aware that this is a conversation about dating you *for show,* not working for you as one of your many interchangeable subordinates at the Korovin Foundation," she said after a moment. "Aren't you?"

"The roles aren't dissimilar."

He stretched his legs out in front of him and lounged even lower in the chair.

"Is this your usual first date checklist, then?"

Her gaze swept over him, and he had no idea what she saw. It surprised him how much he wanted to know.

He nodded, never taking his gaze from hers. "More or less."

"You actually ask a woman to dinner and then present her with this list." She sounded dubious, and something else he wasn't sure he recognized. "Before or after you order starters? And what if she says no? Do you stand up and walk out? Leave her with the bill for her temerity?"

"No one has ever said no." He felt that fire between them reach higher, pull tighter. He could see it on her face. "And I don't take women to dinner without a signed confidentiality agreement. Or anywhere else."

Alicia tapped a finger against her lips for a moment, and he wanted to suck that finger into his own mouth almost more than he wanted his next breath. Need raked through him, raw and hungry.

"You brought me here that night," she pointed out, her tone light, as if there was no tension between them at all. "I certainly didn't sign anything."

Nikolai almost smiled. "You are an anomaly."

"Lucky me," she murmured, faint and dry, and there was no reason that should have worked through him like a match against flint. He didn't like anomalies. He shouldn't have to keep telling himself that.

"If you've absorbed the initial requirements," he said, watching her intently now, "we can move on."

"There are more? The mind boggles."

She was mocking him, he was sure of it. He could see the light of it bright in her eyes and in that wicked twist of her lips, and for some reason, he didn't mind it.

"Sex," he said, and liked the way she froze, for the slightest instant, before concealing her reaction. He had to shift in his seat to hide his.

"You don't really have rules for sex with your girlfriends, Nikolai," she said softly. Imploring him. "Please tell me you're joking."

"I think of this as setting clear boundaries," he told her, leaning forward and smiling when she shivered and sat back. "It prevents undue confusion down the line."

"Undue confusion is what relationships are all about," Alicia said, shaking her head. Her dark eyes searched his, then dropped to her lap. "I rather think that might be the whole point."

"I don't have relationships." He waited until her eyes were on him again, until that tension between them pulled taut and that electric charge was on high, humming through them both. "I have sex. A lot of it. I'll make you come so many times your head will spin, which you already know is no idle boast, but in return, I require two things."

Nikolai watched her swallow almost convulsively, but she didn't look away. She didn't even blink. And he didn't quite know why he felt that like a victory.

"Access and obedience," he said, very distinctly, and was rewarded with the faintest tremor across those lips, down that slender frame. "When I want you, I want you—I don't want a negotiation. Just do what I tell you to do."

He could hear every shift in her breathing. The catch, the slow release. It took every bit of self-control he possessed to wait. To keep his distance. To let her look away for a moment and collect herself, then turn that dark gaze back on him.

"I want to be very clear." She leaned forward, putting her elbows on the table and keeping her eyes trained on him. "What you're telling me, Nikolai, is that every woman pictured on your arm in every single photograph of you online has agreed to all of these *requirements*. All of them."

He wanted to taste her, a violent cut of need, but he didn't. He waited.

"Of course," he said.

And Alicia laughed.

Silvery and musical, just as he remembered. It poured out of her and deep into him, and for a moment he was stunned by it. As if everything disappeared into the sound of it, the way she tipped back her head and let it light up the room. As if she'd hit him from behind and taken him down to the ground without his feeling a single blow.

That laughter rolled into places frozen so solid he'd forgotten they existed at all. It pierced him straight through to a core he hadn't known he had. And it was worse now than it had been that first night. It cut deeper. He was terribly afraid it had made him bleed.

"Laugh as much as you like," he said stiffly when she subsided, and was sitting back in her chair, wiping at her too-bright eyes. "But none of this is negotiable."

"Nikolai," she said, and that clutched at him too, because he'd never heard anyone speak his name like that. So warm, with all of that laughter still moving through her voice. It was almost as if she spoke to someone else entirely, as if it wasn't his name at all—but she looked directly at him, those dark eyes dancing, and he felt as if she'd shot him. He wished she had. He knew how to handle a bullet wound. "I'll play this game of yours. But I'm not going to do any of that."

He was so tense he thought he might simply snap into pieces, but he couldn't seem to move. Her laughter sneaked inside him, messing him up and making even his breathing feel impossibly changed. He hated it.

So he couldn't imagine why he wanted to hear it again, with an intensity that very nearly hurt.

"That's not one of your options," he told her, his voice the roughest he'd ever heard it.

But she was smiling at him, gently, and looked wholly uncowed by his tone.

"If I were you, Nikolai," she said, "I'd start asking myself why I'm so incapable of interacting with other people that I come up with ridiculous rules and regulations to govern things that are supposed to come naturally. That are *better* when they do."

"Because I am a monster," he said. He didn't plan it. It simply came out of his mouth and he did nothing to prevent it. She stopped smiling. Even the brightness in her eyes dimmed. "I've never been anything else. These rules and regulations aren't ridiculous, Alicia. They're necessary."

"Do they make you feel safe?" she asked with a certain quiet kindness he found deeply alarming, as if she knew things she couldn't possibly guess at, much less *know.*

But this was familiar ground even so. He'd had this same conversation with his brother, time and again. He recognized the happy, delusional world she'd come from that let her ask a question like that, and he knew the real world, cynical and bleak. He recognized himself again.

It was a relief, cold and sharp.

"Safety is a delusion," he told her curtly, "and not one I've ever shared. Some of us live our whole lives without succumbing to that particular opiate."

She frowned at him. "Surely when you were a child—"

"I was never a child." He pushed back from the table and rose to his feet. "Not in the way you mean."

She only watched him, still frowning, as he

crossed his arms over his chest, and she didn't move so much as a muscle when he glared down at her. She didn't shrink back the way she should. She looked at him as if he didn't scare her at all, and it ate at him. It made him want to show her how bad he really was—but he couldn't start down that road. He had no idea where it would lead.

"Why do you think my uncle tried to keep me in line with a kitchen knife? It wasn't an accident. He knew what I was."

"Your parents—"

"Died in a fire with seventy others when I was barely five years old," he told her coldly. "I don't remember them. But I doubt they would have liked what I've become. This isn't a bid for sympathy." He shrugged. "It's a truth I accepted a long time ago. Even my own brother believes it, and this after years of being the only one alive who thought I could be any different. I can't." He couldn't look away from her dark eyes, that frown, from the odd and wholly novel notion that she wanted to fight *for* him that opened up a hollow in his chest. "I won't."

"Your brother is an idiot." Her voice was fierce,

as if she was prepared to defend him against Ivan—and even against himself, and he had no idea what to do with that. "Because while families always have some kind of tension, Nikolai, monsters do not exist. No matter what an uncle who holds a knife on a child tells you. No matter what we like to tell ourselves."

"I'm glad you think so." Nikolai wasn't sure he could handle the way she looked at him then, as if she hurt for him. He wasn't sure he knew how. "Soft, breakable creatures like you *should* believe there's nothing terrible out there in the dark. But I know better."

CHAPTER SIX

THAT WAS *PAIN* on his face.

In those searing eyes of his. In the rough scrape of his voice. It was like a dark stain that spilled out from deep inside of him, as if he was torn apart far beneath his strong, icy surface. *Ravaged*, it dawned on her, as surely as if that ferocious thing on his chest rent him to pieces where he stood.

Alicia felt it claw at her, too.

"I'm neither soft nor breakable, Nikolai." She kept her voice steady and her gaze on his, because she thought he needed to see that he hadn't rocked her with that heartbreakingly stark confession, even if he had. "Or as naive as you seem to believe."

"There are four or five ways I could kill you from here." His voice was like gravel. "With my thumb."

Alicia believed him, the way she'd believed he'd be good in bed when he'd told her he was, with a very similar matter-of-fact certainty. It occurred to her that there were any number of ways a man could be talented with his body—with his clever hands for pleasure, with his thumb for something more violent—and Nikolai Korovin clearly knew every one of them. She thought she ought to be frightened by that.

What was wrong with her that she wasn't?

"Please don't," she said briskly, as if she couldn't feel the sting of those claws, as if she didn't see that thick blackness all around him.

Nikolai stared at her. He stood so still, as if he expected he might need to bolt in any direction, and he held himself as if he expected an attack at any moment. As if he expected *she* might be the attacker.

Alicia thought of his coldness tonight, that bone-deep chill that should have hurt, so much harsher than the gruff, darkly amusing man she'd taken by surprise in that club. Who'd surprised her in return. She thought about what little he'd told her of his uncle meant for the boy he must have been—what he must have had to live through. She thought about a man who believed his own brother thought so little of him, and who accepted it as his due. She thought of his lists of rules that he obviously took very seriously indeed, designed to keep even the most intimate people in his life at bay.

I am a monster, he'd said, and she could see that he believed it.

But she didn't. She couldn't.

She ached for him. In a way she was very much afraid—with that little thrill of dark foreboding that prodded at her no matter how she tried to ignore it—would be the end of her. But she couldn't seem to make it stop.

"Nikolai," she said when she couldn't stand it any longer—when she wanted to reach over and touch him, soothe him, and knew she couldn't let herself do that, that *he* wouldn't let her do that anyway, "if you were truly a monster, you would simply *be* one. You wouldn't announce it. You wouldn't know how."

A different expression moved across his face then, the way it had once before in the dark, and tonight it broke her heart. That flash of a vulnerability so deep, so intense. And then she watched him pack it away, cover it in ice, turn it hard and cold.

"There are other things I could do with my thumb," he said, his voice the rough velvet she knew best. Seductive. Demanding. "That wouldn't kill you, necessarily, though you might beg for it before I was done."

But she knew what he was doing. She understood it, and it made her chest hurt.

"Sex is easier to accept than comfort," she said quietly, watching his face as she said it. He looked glacial. Remote. And yet that heat inside of him burned, she could feel it. "You can pretend it's not comfort at all. Just sex."

"I like sex, Alicia." His voice was a harsh lash through the room, so vicious she almost flinched. "I thought I made that clear our first night together. Over and over again."

He wanted to prove he was the monster he said he was. He wanted to prove that he was exactly as bad, as terrifying, as he claimed he was. Capable of killing with nothing more than his thumb. She looked at that cold, set face of his and she could see that he believed it. More—that he simply accepted that this was who he was.

And she found that so terribly sad it almost crippled her.

She got up and went to him without consciously deciding to move. He didn't appear to react, and yet she had the impression he steeled himself at her approach, as if she was as dangerous to him as he was to her. But she couldn't let herself think about that stunning possibility.

Nikolai watched her draw near, his expression even colder. Harder. Alicia tilted her head back and looked into his extraordinary eyes, darker now than usual as he stared back at her with a kind of defiance, as if he was prepared to fight her until she saw him as he saw himself.

Until she called him a monster, too.

"Do you want to know what I think?" she asked.

"I'm certain I don't."

It was a rough scrape of sound, grim and low, but she thought she saw a kind of hunger in his eyes that had nothing to do with his sexual prowess and everything to do with that flash of vulnerability she almost thought she'd imagined, and she kept going.

"I think you hide behind all these rules and boundaries, Nikolai." She felt the air in the room go electric, but she couldn't seem to stop herself. "If you tell yourself you're a monster, if you insist upon it and act upon it, you make it true. It's a self-fulfilling prophecy."

And she would know all about that, wouldn't she? Hadn't she spent eight long years doing exactly that herself? That unexpected insight was like a kick in the stomach, but she ignored it, pushing it aside to look at later.

"Believe me," she said then, more fiercely than she'd intended. "I know."

His hands shot out and took her by the shoulders, then pulled her toward him, toward his hard face that was even more lethal, even more fierce than usual. His touch against her bare arms burned, and made her want nothing more than to melt into him. It was too hot. Too dark.

And he was close then, so powerful and furious. *So close.* Winter and need, fire and longing. The air was thick with it. It made her lungs ache.

"Why don't you have the good sense to be afraid of me?" he said in an undertone, as if the words were torn from that deep, black part of him. "What is the matter with you? Why do you *laugh* when anyone else would cry?"

"I don't see any monsters when I look at you, Nikolai," she replied, winning the fight to keep her tone light, her gaze on his, no matter how ravaged he looked. How undone. Or how churned up she felt inside. "I only see a man. I see you."

His hands tightened around her shoulders for a brief instant, and then he let her go. Abruptly, as if he'd wanted to do the opposite.

As if he couldn't trust himself any more than she could.

"You don't want to play with this particular fire," he warned her, his expression fierce and dark, his gaze drilling holes into her. "It won't simply burn you—it will swallow you whole. That's not a self-fulfilling prophecy. It's an inevitability."

Alicia didn't know what seared through her then, shocking and dark, thrilling to the idea of it. Of truly losing herself in him, in that fire neither one of them could control, despite the fact there was still that panicked part of her—that part of her that wished she'd gone home and done her laundry that night and never met him—that wanted anything but that. And he saw it. All of it.

She had no idea what was happening to her, or how to stop it, or why she had the breathless sense that it was already much too late.

"Get your coat," he growled at her. "I'll take you home."

Alicia blinked, surprised to find that she was unsteady on her own feet. And Nikolai was dark and menacing, watching her as if no detail was too small to escape his notice. As if he could see all those things inside of her, the fire and the need. That dark urge to demand he throw whatever he had at her, that she could take it, that she understood him—

Of course you don't understand him, she chided herself. *How could you?*

"That's unnecessary," she said into the tense silence, stiffly, and had to clear the roughness from her voice with a cough.

She straightened her top, smoothed her hands down the sides of her trousers, then stopped when she realized she was fidgeting and he'd no doubt read the anxiety that betrayed the way he did everything else.

"You don't have to take me home," she said when he didn't respond. When he only watched her, his expression brooding and his blue eyes cold. She frowned at him. "This night has been intense enough, I think. I'll get a taxi."

* * *

The ride across London—in the backseat of Nikolai's SUV with him taking up too much of the seat beside her because he'd informed her a taxi was not an option—was much like sitting on simmering coals, waiting for the fire to burst free.

Not exactly comfortable, Alicia thought crossly. And as the fever of what had happened between them in his penthouse faded with every mile they traveled, she realized he'd been right to warn her.

She felt scorched through. Blackened around the edges and much too close to simply going up in flames herself, until she very much feared there'd be nothing left of her. A few ashes, scattered here and there.

Had she really stood there thinking she wanted more of this? Anything he had to give, in fact? What *was* the matter with her?

But then she thought of that bleak look in his beautiful eyes, that terrible certainty in his voice when he'd told her what a monster he was, and she was afraid she knew all too well what was wrong with her.

"You can go," she told him, not bothering to hide the tension in her voice as they stood outside the door that led into her building in a narrow alcove stuck between two darkened shops.

Nikolai had walked her to the door without a word, that winter fire roaring all around them both, and now stood close beside her in the chilly December night. Too close beside her. Alicia needed to get inside, lock her doors, take a very long soak in the bath—*something* to sort her head out before she lost whatever remained of her sanity, if not something far worse than that. *She needed him to go.* She dug for her keys in her bag without looking at him, not trusting herself to look away again if she did.

"I'm fine from here. I don't need an escort."

He didn't respond. He plucked the keys from her hand when she pulled them out, and then opened the door with no hesitation whatsoever, waving her inside with a hint of edgy impatience.

It would not be wise to let him in. That was perfectly clear to her.

"Nikolai," she began, and his gaze slammed into her, making her gulp down whatever she might have said.

"I understand that you need to fight me on everything," he said, his accent thicker than usual.

"If I wanted to psychoanalyze you the way you did me, I'd say I suspect it makes you feel powerful to poke at me. But I wouldn't get too comfortable with that if I were you."

"I wasn't psychoanalyzing you!" she cried, but he brushed it off as if she hadn't spoken.

"But you should ask yourself something." He put his hand on her arm and hauled her into the building, sent the door slamming shut with the back of his shoulder and then held her there in the narrow hall. "Exactly what do you think might happen if you get what you seem to want and I lose control?"

"I don't want—"

"There are reasons men control themselves," he told her, his face in hers, and she should have been intimidated. She should have been terrified. And instead, all she felt was that greedy pulse of need roll through her. That impossible kick of this jagged-edged joy he brought out in her no matter what she thought she *ought* to feel. "Especially men like me, who stand like wolves in the dark corners of more than just London clubs. You should think about what those reasons are. There are far worse things than a list of demands."

"Like your attempts to intimidate me?" she countered, trying to find her footing when she was so off balance she suspected she might have toppled over without him there to hold her up.

"Why don't you laugh it off?" he asked softly, more a taunt than a question, and she had the wild thought that this might be Nikolai at his most dangerous. Soft and deadly and much too close. His gaze brushed over her face, leaving ice and fire wherever it touched. "No? Is this not funny anymore?"

"Nikolai." His name felt unwieldy against her tongue, or perhaps that was the look in his eyes, spelling out her sure doom in all of that ferocious blue. "I'm not trying to make you lose control."

"Oh, I think you are." He smiled, though it was almost feral and it scraped over her, through her. "But you should make very, very sure that you're prepared to handle the consequences if you succeed. Do you think you are? Right here in this hallway, with a draft under the door and the street a step away? Do you think you're ready for that?"

"Stop threatening me," she bit out at him, but it was a ragged whisper, and he could see into her too easily.

"I don't make threats, Alicia." He leaned in closer and nipped at her neck, shocking her. Making her go up in flames. And flinch—or was that simply an electric charge? "You should think of that, too."

And then he stepped away and jerked his head in an unspoken demand that she lead him up the stairs. And Alicia was so unsteady, so chaotic inside, so unable to process all the things that had happened tonight—what he'd said, what she'd felt, that deep ache inside of her, that fire that never did anything but burn hotter—that she simply marched up the stairs to the flat she shared with Rosie on the top floor without a word of protest.

He didn't ask if she wanted him inside when they reached her door, he simply strode in behind her as if he owned the place, and the insanity of it—of *Nikolai Korovin* standing there *in her home*—was so excruciating it was like pain.

"I don't want you here," she told him as he shut her door behind him, the sound of the latch engaging and locking him inside with her too loud in her ears. "I didn't invite you in."

"I didn't ask."

He was still dressed in black, and that very

darkness made him seem bigger and more lethal as he walked inside, his cold gaze moving over the cheerful clutter that was everywhere. Bright paperbacks shoved haphazardly onto groaning shelves, photographs in colorful frames littering every surface, walls painted happy colors and filled with framed prints of famous art from around the world. Alicia tensed, expecting Rosie to pad into view at any moment, but the continuing stretch of silence suggested she was out. *Thank God.*

"It's messy," she said, aware she sounded defensive. "We never quite get around to cleaning it as we should. Of course, we also don't have a household staff."

"It looks like real people live here," he replied, frowning at one of Rosie's abandoned knitting projects, and it took her a moment to understand that this, too, was a terribly sad thing to say.

That ache in her deepened. Expanded. Hurt.

Alicia tossed her keys on the table in the hall, her coat over the chair, and then followed Nikolai warily as he melted in and out of the rooms of the flat like a shadow.

"What are you looking for?" she asked after a few minutes of this.

"There must be a reason you're suicidally incapable of recognizing your own peril when you see it," he said, his eyes moving from place to place, object to object, taking everything in. Cataloging it, she thought. Examining every photograph the way he did every dish left in the sink, every pair of shoes kicked aside in the hall, and the spine of every book piled on the overstuffed bookshelves. "Perhaps there are environmental factors at play."

He moved past the kitchen off to the right and stood at the far end of the hall that cut down the middle of the flat, where the bedrooms were.

"And what would those be, do you think?" she asked, her voice tart—which felt like a vast improvement. Or was perhaps a response to what had sounded like the faintest hint of that dark humor of his. It was absurd how much she craved more of it. "Fearlessness tucked away in the walls like asbestos?"

Nikolai didn't answer her, he only sent one of those simmering looks arrowing her way down the hallway, as effective from a few feet away as it was up close. And almost as devastating.

Alicia blew out a breath when he opened the door to her bedroom, the aftershocks of that winter-blue look shifting into something else again. A kind of nervous anticipation. He looked inside for a long moment, and her heart raced. She wished, suddenly, that she'd had the presence of mind to prevent this. She didn't like the fact that he knew, now, that she favored all those silly, self-indulgent throw pillows, piled so high on her bed, shouting out how soft and breakable she really was. They felt like proof, somehow—and when he looked back at her it was hard to stand still. To keep from offering some kind of explanation.

"A four-poster bed." It could have been an innocent comment. An observation. But the way he looked at her made her knees feel weak. "Intriguing."

Alicia thought she understood then, and somehow, that eased the relentless pulse of panic inside.

"Let me guess." She leaned her hip against the wall and watched him. "The faster you puzzle me out, the less you think you'll have to worry about losing this control of yours."

"I don't like mysteries."

"Will it make you feel safe to solve whatever

mystery you think I am, Nikolai? Is that what this is?"

The look he gave her then did more than simply *hurt*. It ripped straight down into the center of her, tearing everything she was in two, and there was nothing she could do but stand there and take it.

"I'm not the one who believes in safety, Alicia," he said softly. "It's nothing more than a fairy tale to me. I never had it. I wouldn't recognize it." His expression was hard and bleak. Almost challenging. "The next time you tally up my scars, keep a special count of those I got when I was under the age of twelve. That knife was only one among many that drew my blood. My uncle used the back of his hand if I was lucky." His beautiful mouth twisted, and her heart dropped to her feet. "But I was never very lucky."

He stood taller then. Almost defiant. And it tore at her. She felt her eyes heat in a way that spelled imminent tears and knew she couldn't let herself cry for this hard, damaged man. Not where he could see it. She knew somehow that he would never forgive her.

"Don't waste your pity on me." His voice was cold, telling her she'd been right. No sympathy allowed. No compassion. He sounded almost insulted when he continued, as if whatever he saw on her face was a slap. "Eventually, I learned how to fight back, and I became more of a monster than my uncle ever could have been."

"We're all monsters," she told him, her voice harsh because she knew he wouldn't accept anything softer. Hoping against hope he'd never know about that great tear inside of her that she could feel with every breath she took, rending her further and further apart. "Some of us actually behave like monsters, in fact, rather than suffer through the monstrous actions of others. No one escapes their past unscathed."

"What would you know about it, Alicia?" His gaze was cold, his tone a stinging lash. "What past misdeeds could possibly haunt you while you're tucked up in your virginal little bedroom, laughing your way through your cheery, happy life? What blood do you imagine is on your hands?"

And so she told him.

Alicia had never told a soul before, and yet she told Nikolai as easily as if she'd shared the story a thousand times. Every detail she could remember and all the ones she couldn't, that her father had filled in for her that awful morning. All of her shame, her despicable actions, her unforgivable behavior, without garnishment or pretense. As if that tear in her turned her inside out, splayed there before him.

And when she was finished, she was so light-headed she thought she might sag straight down to the floor, or double over where she stood.

"Everyone has ghosts," she managed to say, crossing her arms over her chest to keep herself upright.

Nikolai turned away from her bedroom door and moved toward her, thrusting his hands into the pockets of his trousers as he did. It made him look more dangerous, not less. It drew her attention to the wide strength of his shoulders, the long, lethal lines of his powerful frame. It made her wonder how anyone could have hurt him so badly when he'd been small that he'd felt he needed to transform himself into so sharp, so deadly a weapon. It made her feel bruised to the core that he'd no doubt look at her now the way her father had....

His eyes burned as they bored into hers, and he let out one of those low laughs that made her stomach tense.

"That doesn't sound like any ghost," he said, his voice dark and sure. "It sounds like an older man who took advantage of a young girl too drunk to fight him off."

Alicia jolted cold, then flashed hot, as he turned her entire life on end that easily. She swayed where she stood.

"No," she said, feeling desperate, as some great wave of terror or emotion or *something* rolled toward her. "My father said—"

"Your father should have known better than to speak to you like that." Nikolai scowled at her. "News flash, Alicia. Men who aren't predators prefer to have sex with women who are capable of participating."

Her head was spinning. Her stomach twisted, and for a panicked moment she thought she might be sick. She felt his words—so matter-of-fact, as if there could be no other interpretation of that night, much less the one that she'd held so close all these years—wash through her, like a quiet and devastating tsunami right there in her own hallway.

"What's his name?" Nikolai asked, in that soft, lethal way of his that lifted the hairs at the back of her neck. "The man who did these things to you? Does he still live next door to your parents?"

He was the first person she'd told. And the only one to defend her.

Alicia couldn't understand how she was still standing upright.

"That doesn't sound like a question a monster would ask," she whispered.

"You don't know what I'd do to him," he replied, that dark gleam in his gaze.

And he looked at her like she was important, not filthy. Not a whore. Like what had happened had been done to *her*, and hadn't been something *she'd* done.

Like it wasn't her fault after all.

She couldn't breathe.

His gaze shifted from hers to a spot down at the other end of the flat behind her, and she heard the jingling of keys in the hall outside. She felt as if she moved through sticky syrup, as if her body didn't understand what to do any longer, and turned around just as Rosie pushed her way inside.

Rosie sang out her usual hello, slinging her bags to the floor. Nikolai stepped closer to Alicia's back, then reached around to flatten his hand against the waistband of her trousers before pulling her into his bold heat. Holding her to his chest as if they were lovers. Claiming her.

"What…?" Alicia whispered, the sizzle of that unexpected touch combining with the hard punch of the revolution he'd caused inside of her, making her knees feel weak.

"I told you we were taking this public," he replied, his voice a low rumble pitched only to her that made her shiver helplessly against him. "Now we have."

Rosie's head snapped up at the sound of his voice. Her mouth made a perfect, round O as if the devil himself stood there behind Alicia in the hall, no doubt staring her down with those cold winter eyes of his. And then she dropped the bottle of wine she'd been holding in her free hand, smashing it into a thousand pieces all over the hall floor.

Which was precisely how Alicia felt.

Nikolai stared out at the wet and blustery London night on the other side of his penthouse's windows while he waited for the video conference with Los

Angeles to begin. His office was reflected in the glass, done in imposing blacks and burgundies, every part of it carefully calculated to trumpet his wealth and power without him having to say a word to whoever walked in. The expensive view out of all the windows said it for him. The modern masterpieces on the walls repeated it, even louder.

It was the sort of thing he'd used to take such pleasure in. The application of his wealth and power to the most innocuous of interactions, the leverage it always afforded him. War games without a body count. It had been his favorite sport for years.

But now he thought only of the one person who seemed as unimpressed with these trappings of wealth and fame as she did with the danger he was well aware he represented. Hell, *exuded.* And instead of regaining his equilibrium the more time he spent with Alicia, instead of losing this intense and distracting interest in her the more he learned about her, he was getting worse.

Much worse. Incomprehensibly worse. And Nikolai knew too well what it felt like to spiral. He knew what obsession tasted like. *He knew.*

She was a latter-day version of his favorite

drink, sharp and deadly. And he was still nothing but a drunk where she was concerned.

He'd ordered himself not to hunt down the man who had violated her, though he knew it would be easy. Too easy. The work of a single phone call, an internet search.

You are not her protector, he told himself over and over. *This is not your vengeance to take.*

He'd sparred for hours with his security team in his private gym, throwing them to the floor one after the next, punching and kicking and flipping. He'd swum endless laps in his pool. He'd run through the streets of London in the darkest hours of the night, the slap of the December weather harsh against his face, until his lungs burned and his legs shook.

Nothing made the slightest bit of difference. Nothing helped.

She'd all but pushed him out her front door that night, past her gaping flatmate and the wine soaking into her floorboards, her eyes stormy and dark, and he'd let her.

"Rosie calls me *Saint Alicia* and I *like* it," she'd whispered fiercely to him, shoving him into the narrow hall outside her flat. She'd been scolding him, he'd realized. He wasn't sure he'd ever experienced it before. His uncle had preferred to use his belt. "It's better than some other things I've been called. But you looming around the flat will be the end of that."

"Why?" he'd asked lazily, those broken, jagged things moving around inside of him, making him want things he couldn't name. Making him want to hurt anyone who'd dared hurt her, like she was his. "I like saints. I'm Russian."

"Please," she'd scoffed. "You have 'corruptor of innocents' written all over you."

"Then we are both lucky, are we not, that neither one of us is innocent," he'd said, and had enjoyed the heat that had flashed through her eyes, chasing out the dark.

But by the next morning, she'd built her walls back up, and higher than before. He hadn't liked that at all, though he'd told himself it didn't matter. It shouldn't matter. He told himself that again, now.

It was the end result he needed to focus on: Veronika. The truth about Stefan at long last, and the loose thread she represented snipped off for good. Whatever he suffered on the way to that goal would be worth it, and in any case, Alicia would soon be nothing but a memory. One more instrument he'd use as he needed, then set aside.

He needed to remember that. There was only a week left before the ball. Nikolai could handle anything for one last week, surely. He'd certainly handled worse.

But she was under his skin, he knew, no matter how many times he told himself otherwise. No matter how fervently he pretended she wasn't.

And she kept clawing her way deeper, like a wound that wouldn't scar over and become one more thing he'd survived.

He'd picked her up to take her to the Tate Modern on the opening night of some desperately chic exhibit, which he'd known would be teeming with London's snooty art world devotees and their assorted parasites and photographers. It wasn't the kind of place a man took a woman he kept around only for sex. Taking a woman to a highly intellectual and conceptual art exhibit suggested he might actually have an interest in her thoughts.

It was a perfect place for them to be "accidentally spotted," in other words. Nikolai hadn't wanted to dig too deeply into his actual level of interest in what went on inside her head. He hadn't wanted to confront himself.

Alicia had swung open the door to her flat and taken his breath that easily. She'd worn a skimpy red dress that showed off her perfect breasts and clung to her curves in mouthwatering ways he would have enjoyed on any woman, and deeply appreciated on her—and yet he'd had the foreign urge to demand she hide all of her lush beauty away from the undeserving public. That she keep it for him alone. He'd been so startled—and appalled—at his line of thought that he'd merely stood there, silent and grim, and stared at her as if she'd gone for his jugular with one of her wickedly high shoes.

Alicia had taken in the black sweater with the high collar he wore over dark trousers that, he'd been aware, made him look more like a commando than an appropriately urbane date to a highly anticipated London art exhibit.

Not that commandos wore cashmere, in his experience.

"Have you become some kind of spy?" she'd asked him, in that dry way that might as well have been her hands on his sex. His body hadn't been at all conflicted about how he should figure her out. It had known exactly what it wanted.

When it came to Alicia, he'd realized, it always did.

"You must be confusing me for the character my brother plays in movies," he'd told her dismissively, and had fought to keep himself from simply leaning forward and pressing his mouth to that tempting hollow between her breasts, then licking his way over each creamy brown swell until he'd made them both delirious and hot. He'd almost been able to taste her from where he stood in the doorway.

Alicia had pulled on her coat from the nearby chair and swept her bag into her hand. She hadn't even been looking at him as she stepped out into the hall and turned to lock her door behind her.

"Your brother plays you in his Jonas Dark films," she'd replied in that crisp way of hers that made his skin feel tight against his bones. "A disaffected kind of James Bond character, stretched too thin on the edge of what's left of his humanity, yet called to act the hero despite himself."

Nikolai had stared at her when she'd turned to face him, and she'd stared back, that awareness and a wary need moving across her expressive face, no doubt reflecting his own. Making him wish—

But he'd known he had to stop. He'd known better from the first with her, hadn't he? He should have let her fall to the floor in that club. He'd known it even as he'd caught her.

"I'm no hero, Alicia," he'd said, sounding like sandpaper and furious that she'd pushed him off balance again. Hadn't he warned her what would happen? Was that what she wanted? She didn't know what she was asking—but he did. "Surely you know this better than anyone."

She'd looked at him for a long moment, her dark gaze shrewd, seeing things he'd always wanted nothing more than to hide.

"Maybe not," she'd said. "But what do you think would happen if you found out you were wrong?"

And then she'd turned and started down the stairs toward the street, as if she hadn't left the shell of him behind her, hollow and unsettled.

Again.

Nikolai saw his own reflection in his office windows now, and it was like he was someone else. He was losing control and he couldn't seem to stop it. He was as edgy and paranoid and dark as he'd been in those brutal days after he'd quit drinking. Worse, perhaps.

Because these things that raged in him, massive and uncontrollable and hot like acid, were symptoms of a great thaw he knew he couldn't allow. A thaw she was making hotter by the day, risking everything. Oceans rose when glaciers melted; mountains fell.

He'd destroy her, he knew. It was only a matter of time.

If he was the man she seemed to think he was, the man he sometimes wished he was when she looked at him with all of those things he couldn't name in her lovely dark eyes, he'd leave her alone. Play the hero she'd suggested he could be and put her out of harm's way.

But Nikolai knew he'd never been any kind of hero. Not even by mistake.

CHAPTER SEVEN

NIKOLAI HADN'T HEARD his family nickname in such a long time that when he did, he assumed he'd imagined it.

He frowned at the sleek and oversize computer display in front of him, realizing that he'd barely paid attention to the video conference, which was unlike him. Stranger still, no one remained on his screen but his brother.

Nikolai wasn't sure which was more troubling, his inattention during a business meeting or the fact he'd imagined he'd heard Ivan speak his—

"Kolya?"

That time there was no mistaking it. Ivan was the only person alive who had ever used that name, very rarely at that, and Nikolai was looking right at him as he said it from the comfort of his Malibu house a world away.

It was the first time he'd spoken directly to Nikolai in more than two years.

Nikolai stared. Ivan was still Ivan. Dark eyes narrowed beneath the dark hair they shared, the battered face he'd earned in all of those mixed martial arts rings, clothes that quietly proclaimed him Hollywood royalty, every inch of him the action hero at his ease.

Nikolai would have preferred it if Ivan had fallen into obvious disrepair after turning his back on his only brother so cavalierly. Instead, it appeared that betrayal and delusion suited him.

That, Nikolai reflected darkly, and the woman who'd caused this rift between them in the first place, no doubt.

"What's the matter with you?" Ivan asked in Russian, frowning into his camera. "You've been staring off into space for the past fifteen minutes."

Nikolai chose not to investigate the things that churned in him, dark and heavy, at the way Ivan managed to convey the worry, the disappointment and that particular wariness that had always characterized the way he looked at Nikolai, talked to him, in two simple sentences after so much silence. And yet there was a part of him that wanted nothing more than to simply take this as a gift, take his brother back in whatever way Ivan was offering himself....

But he couldn't let himself go there. Ivan's silence had been a favor to him, surely. He knew where it led, and he wanted nothing to do with that particular prison any longer.

"I'm reeling from shock," he said. "The mighty Ivan Korovin has condescended to address me directly. I imagine I ought to feel festive on such a momentous occasion." He eyed Ivan coolly, and without the faintest hint of *festive*. "I appreciate the show of concern, of course."

Nikolai could have modified his tone, the sardonic slap of it. Instead, he kept his face expressionless, his gaze trained on his brother through the screen. *Your brother is an idiot,* Alicia had said, so emphatically. It felt like encouragement, like her kind hand against his cheek even when she wasn't in the room.

But he didn't want to think about Alicia. She didn't know what he'd done to deserve the things his brother thought of him. And unlike her confession of the sins of others, Nikolai really had done each and every thing Ivan thought he had.

Ivan's mouth flattened and his dark eyes flashed with his familiar temper.

"Two years," he said in that gruff way of his, his long-suffering older brother voice, "and that's what you have to say to me, Nikolai? Why am I not surprised that you've learned nothing in all this time?"

"That's an excellent question," Nikolai replied, his voice so cold he could feel the chill of it in his own chest. "If you wanted me to learn something you should have provided some kind of lesson plan. Picked out the appropriate hair shirts for me to wear, outlined the confessions you expected me to make and at what intervals. But you chose instead to disappear, the way you always do." He shrugged, only spurred on by the flash of guilt and fury he knew too well on his brother's face. "Forgive me if I am not weeping with joy that you've remembered I exist, with as much warning as when you decided to forget it." He paused, then if possible, got icier. *"Brother."*

"Nikolai—"

"You come and you go, Vanya," he said then, giving that darkness in him free rein. Letting it take him over. Not caring that it wasn't fair—what was *fair?* What had ever been *fair?* "You make a thousand promises and you break them all. I stopped depending on you when I was a child. Talk to me or don't talk to me. What is it to me?"

Ivan's face was dark with that same complicated fury—his guilt that he'd left Nikolai years before to fight, his frustrated anger that Nikolai had turned out so relentlessly feral despite the fact he'd rescued him, eventually; even his sadness that this was who they were, these two hard and dangerous men—and Nikolai was still enough his younger brother to read every nuance of that. And to take a kind of pleasure in the fact that despite the passage of all this time, Ivan was not indifferent.

Which, he was aware, meant he wasn't, either.

"One of these days, little brother, we're going to fight this out," Ivan warned him, shoving his hands through his dark hair the way he'd no doubt like to shove them around Nikolai's neck and would have, had this conversation taken place in person. Nikolai felt himself shift into high alert, readying for battle automatically. "No holds barred, the way we should have done two years ago. And when I crush you into the ground, and

I will, this conversation will be one of the many things you'll apologize for."

"Is that another promise?" Nikolai asked point-edly, and was rewarded when Ivan winced. "I understand this is your pet fantasy and always has been. And you could no doubt win a fight in any ring, to entertain a crowd. But outside the ring? In real life with real stakes?" Nikolai shook his head. "You'd be lucky to stay alive long enough to beg for mercy."

"Why don't you fly to California and test that theory?" Ivan suggested, his expression turning thunderous. "Or is it easier to say these things when there are computer screens and whole continents to hide behind?"

"You would follow the rules, Vanya," Nikolai said with a certain grim impatience. "You would fight fair, show mercy. This is who you are." He shrugged, everything inside of him feeling too sharp, too jagged. "It will be your downfall."

"Mercy isn't weakness," Ivan growled.

"Only good men, decent men, have the luxury of dispensing it," Nikolai retorted, ignoring the way his brother stared at him. "I wouldn't make that kind of mistake. You might put me on the ground, but I'd sink a knife in you on my way back up. You should remember that while you're issuing threats. I don't fight fair. I fight to survive."

They stared at each other for an uncomfortable moment. Ivan settled back in his chair, crossing his strong arms over his massive chest, and Nikolai sat still and watchful, like the sentry he'd once been.

"Is this about your new woman?" Ivan asked. Nikolai didn't betray his surprise by so much as a twitch of his eyelid, much less a reply. Ivan sighed. "I've seen the papers."

"So I gather."

Ivan studied him for another moment. "She's not your usual type."

"By which you mean vapid and/or mercenary, I presume," Nikolai said coldly. He almost laughed. "No, she's not. But you of all people should know better than to believe the things you read."

Ivan's gaze on his became curiously intent.

"Tabloid games don't always lead where you think they will, brother. You know that."

It was Nikolai's turn to sigh. "And how is your favorite tabloid game gone wrong?" he asked.

"Your wife now, if I'm not mistaken. Or so I read in the company newsletter."

"Miranda is fine," Ivan said shortly, and then looked uncomfortable, that guilty look flashing through his dark eyes again. "It was a very private ceremony. No one but the man who married us."

"I understand completely," Nikolai murmured smoothly. "It might have been awkward to have to explain why your only living family member, the acting CEO of your foundation, was not invited to a larger wedding. It might have tarnished your image, which, of course, would cost us all money. Can't have that."

"She's my family, Kolya." Ivan's voice was a hard rumble, his jaw set in that belligerent way of his that meant he was ready to fight. Here and now.

And that really shouldn't have felt like one of his brother's trademark punches, a sledgehammer to the side of the head. It shouldn't have surprised him that Ivan considered that woman his family when he'd so easily turned his back on his only actual blood relation. Or that he was prepared to fight Nikolai—again—to defend her.

And yet he felt leveled. Laid out flat, no air in his lungs.

"Congratulations," he ground out. Dark and bitter. Painful. "I hope your new family proves less disappointing than the original version you were so happy to discard."

Ivan wasn't the only one who could land a blow.

Nikolai watched him look away from the screen, and rub one of his big hands over his hard face. He even heard the breath that Ivan took, then blew out, and knew his brother was struggling to remain calm. That should have felt like a victory.

"I know you feel that I abandoned you," Ivan said after a moment, in his own, painful way. "That everyone did, but in my case, over and over, when you were the most vulnerable. I will always wish I could change that."

Nikolai couldn't take any more of this. Ice floes were cracking apart inside of him, turning into so much water and flooding him, drowning him— and he couldn't allow this to happen. He didn't know where it was heading, or what would be left of him when he melted completely. He only knew it wouldn't be pretty. For anyone. He'd always known that. The closest he'd ever been to *melted* was drunk, and that had only ever ended in blood and regret.

"It's only been two years, Ivan." He tried to pull himself back together, to remember who he was, or at least pretend well enough to end this conversation. "I haven't suddenly developed a host of tender emotions you need to concern yourself with trampling."

"You have emotions, Nikolai. You just can't handle them," Ivan corrected him curtly, a knife sliding in neat and hard. Deep enough to hit bone. His eyes were black and intense, and they slammed into Nikolai from across the globe with all of his considerable power. "You never learned how to have them, much less process them, so your first response when you feel something is to attack. Always."

"Apparently things *have* changed," Nikolai shot back with icy fury. "I wasn't aware you'd followed your wife's example and become no better than a tabloid reporter, making up little fantasies and selling them as fact. I hope the tips of the trade you get in bed are worth the loss of self-respect."

"Yes, Nikolai," Ivan bit out, short and hard. "Exactly like that."

Nikolai muttered dark things under his breath, fighting to keep that flood inside of him under control. Not wanting to think about what his brother had said, or why it seemed to echo in him, louder and louder. Why he had Alicia's voice in his head again, talking about sex and comfort in that maddeningly intuitive way of hers, as if she knew, too, the ways he reacted when he didn't know how to feel.

Did he ever know how to feel?

And Ivan only settled back in his chair, crossing his arms over his chest, and watched Nikolai fall apart.

"I'm the thing that goes bump in the night," Nikolai said through his teeth after a moment or two. "You know this. I've never pretended to be anything else."

"Because our uncle told you so?" Ivan scoffed. "Surely you must realize by now that he was in love with our mother in his own sick way. He hated us both for representing the choice she made, but you—" He shook his head. "Your only sin was in resembling her more than I did."

Nikolai couldn't let that in. He couldn't let it land. Because it was nothing but misdirection and psychological inference when he knew the truth. He'd learned it the hard way, hadn't he?

"I know what I am," he gritted out.

"You like it." Ivan's gaze was hard. No traces of any guilt now. "I think it comforts you to imagine you're an irredeemable monster, unfit for any kind of decent life."

You make it true, Alicia had told him, her dark eyes filled with soft, clear things he hadn't known how to define. *It's a self-fulfilling prophecy.*

"You think it yourself," Nikolai reminded Ivan tightly. "Or did I misunderstand your parting words two years ago?"

"If I thought that," Ivan rumbled at him, "I wouldn't think you could do better than this, would I? But you don't want to accept that, Nikolai, because if you did, you'd have to take responsibility for your actions." He held Nikolai's gaze. "Like a man."

I only see a man, Alicia had told him, her dark gaze serious. *I see you.*

But that wasn't what Nikolai saw. Not in the mirror, not in Alicia's pretty eyes, not in his brother's face now. He saw the past.

He saw the truth.

He'd been nine years old. Ivan had been off winning martial arts tournaments already, and Nikolai had borne the brunt of one of his uncle's drunken rages, as usual.

He'd been lucky the teeth he'd lost were only the last of his milk teeth.

"I can see it in you," his uncle had shouted at him, over and over again, fists flying. "It looks out of your eyes."

He'd towered over Nikolai's bed, Nikolai's blood on his hands and splattered across his graying white shirt. That was the part Nikolai always remembered so vividly, even now—that spray of red that air and time had turned brown, set deep in the grungy shirt that his uncle had never bothered to throw out. That he'd worn for years afterward, like a promise.

His uncle had always kept his promises. Every last one, every time, until his nephews grew big enough to make a few of their own.

"Soon there'll be nothing left," his uncle had warned him, his blue eyes, so much like Nikolai's, glittering. "That thing in you will be all you are."

Ivan hadn't come home for days. Nikolai had thought that his uncle had finally succeeded in killing him, that he'd been dying. By the time Ivan returned and had quietly, furiously, cleaned him up, Nikolai had changed.

He'd understood.

There was nothing good in him. If there had been, his uncle wouldn't have had to beat him so viciously, so consistently, the way he had since Nikolai had come to live with him at five years old.

It was his fault his uncle had no choice but to beat the bad things out.

It was his fault, or someone would have rescued him.

It was his fault, or it would stop. But it wouldn't stop, because that thing inside of him was a monster and eventually, he'd understood then, it would take him over. Wholly and completely.

And it had.

"Nikolai."

Maybe Ivan had been right to sever this connection, he thought now. What did they have between them besides terrible memories of those dark, bloody years? Of course Ivan hadn't protected him, no matter how Nikolai had prayed he might—he'd barely managed to protect himself.

And now he'd made himself a real family, without these shadows. Without all of that blood between them.

"Kolya—"

"I can't tell you how much I appreciate this brotherly talk," Nikolai said, his tone arctic. Because it was the only way he knew to protect Ivan. And if Nikolai could give that to him, he would, for every bruise and cut and broken bone that Ivan had stoically tended to across the years. "I've missed this. Truly."

And then he reached out and cut off the video connection before his brother could say another word. But not before he saw that same, familiar sadness in Ivan's eyes. He'd seen it all his life.

He knew it hurt Ivan that this was who Nikolai was. That nothing had changed, and nothing ever would.

Ivan was wrong. Nikolai *was* changing, and it wasn't for the better. It was a terrible thing, that flood inside him swelling and rising by the second, making all of that ice he'd wrapped himself in melt down much too quickly.

He was changing far more than he should.

Far more than was safe for anyone.

He knew he needed to stop it, he knew how, and yet he couldn't bring himself to do it. At his core, he was nothing but that twisted, evil thing who had earned his uncle's fists.

Because he wasn't ready to give her up. He had a week left, a week of that marvelous smile and the way she frowned at him without a scrap of fear, a week of that wild heat he needed to sample one more time before he went without it forever. He wanted every last second of it.

Even if it damned them both.

Alicia stood in a stunning hotel suite high above the city of Prague, watching it glow in the last of the late-December afternoon, a storybook kingdom brought to life before her. Snow covered the picturesque red rooftops and clung to the spires atop churches and castles, while the ancient River Vltava curved like a sweet silver ribbon through the heart of it. She listened as bells tolled out joyful melodies from every side, and reminded herself—again—that she wasn't the princess in this particular fairy tale, despite appearances to the contrary.

That Nikolai had told her the night he'd met her that it would end in teeth. And tears.

The charity Christmas ball was the following night, where he would have that conversation with his ex-wife at last, and after that it wouldn't matter how perfect Prague looked, how achingly lovely its cobbled streets or its famous bridges bristling with Gothic saints. It didn't matter how golden it seemed in the winter sunset, how fanciful, as if it belonged on a gilded page in an ancient manuscript. She would leave this city as she'd found it, and this agonizing charade would end. Nikolai would get what he wanted and she would get her life back.

She should want that, she knew. She should be thrilled.

If she stuck her head out her door she could hear the low rumble of Nikolai's voice from somewhere else in the great, ornate hotel suite he'd chosen, all golds and reds and plush Bohemian extravagance. He was on a call, taking care of business in that ruthless way of his. Because he didn't allow distractions—he'd told her so himself.

Not foreign cities that looked too enchanted to be real. Certainly not her.

And Alicia was in a room that was twice the size of her flat and a hundred times more lush, one deep breath away from losing herself completely to the things she was still afraid to let herself feel lest she simply explode across the floor like that bottle of wine, practicing her prettiest smile against the coming dark.

None of this was real, she reminded herself, tracing her finger across the cold glass of the window. None of this was hers.

In the end, none of it would matter.

The only thing that would remain of these strange weeks were the pictures in the tabloids, stuck on the internet forever like her very own scarlet letter. There would be no record of the way she ached for him. There would be no evidence that she'd ever felt her heart tear open, or that long after he'd left that night, she'd cried into her mountain of frilly pillows for a scared little boy with bright blue eyes who'd never been lucky or safe. And for the girl she'd been eight years ago, who only Nikolai had ever tried to defend from an attack she couldn't even remember. No one would know if she healed or not, because no one would know she'd been hurt.

There would only be those pictures and the non-existent relationship Nikolai had made sure they showed to the world, that she'd decided she no longer cared if her father knew about.

Let him think what he likes, she'd thought.

Alicia had taken the train out for his birthday dinner the previous week, and had sat with her sisters around the table in his favorite local restaurant, pretending everything was all right. The way she always pretended it was.

But not because she'd still been racked with shame, as she'd been for all those years. Instead, she'd realized as she'd watched her father *not* look at her and *not* acknowledge her and she understood at last what had actually happened to her, she'd been a great deal closer to furious.

"Will you have another drink, love?" her mother had asked her innocuously enough, but Alicia had been watching her father. She'd seen him wince at the very idea, as if another glass of wine would have Alicia doffing her clothes in the middle of the King's Arms. And all of that fury and pain and all of those terrible years fused inside of her. She'd been as unable to keep quiet as she'd been when she'd told Nikolai about this mess in the first place.

"No need to worry, Dad," she'd said brusquely. "I haven't been anywhere close to drunk in years. Eight years to be precise. And would you like to know why?"

He'd stared at her, then looked around at the rest of the family, all of them gaping from him to Alicia and back.

"No need," he'd said sharply. "I'm already aware."

"I was so drunk I couldn't walk," she'd told him, finally. "I take full responsibility for that. My friends poured me into a taxi and it took me ages to make it up to the house from the lane. I didn't want to wake anyone, so I went into the garden and lay down to sleep beneath the stars."

"For God's sake, Alicia!" her father had rumbled. "This isn't the time or place to bring up this kind of—"

"I passed out," she'd retorted, and she'd been perfectly calm. Focused. "I can't remember a single thing about it because I was *unconscious*. And yet when you saw Mr. Reddick helping himself to your comatose daughter, the conclusion you reached was that I was a whore."

There'd been a long, highly charged silence.

"He tried it on with me, too," her older sister had declared at last, thumping her drink down on the tabletop. "Vile pervert."

"I always thought he wasn't right," her other sister had chimed in at almost the same moment. "Always staring up at our windows, peering through the hedge."

"I had no idea," her mother had said urgently then, reaching over and taking hold of Alicia's hand, squeezing it tightly in hers. Then she'd frowned at her husband. "Bernard, you should be ashamed of yourself! Douglas Reddick was a menace to every woman in the village!"

And much later, after they'd all talked themselves blue and teary while her father had sat there quietly, and Douglas Reddick's sins had been thoroughly documented, her father had hugged her goodbye for the first time in nearly a decade. His form of an apology, she supposed.

And much as she'd wanted to rail at him further, she hadn't. Alicia had felt that great big knot she'd carried around inside of her begin to loosen, and she'd let it, because she'd wanted her father back more than she'd wanted to be angry.

She'd have that to carry with her out of her fake relationship. And surely that was something. Only she would know who had helped her stand up for herself eight years later. Only she would remember the things he'd changed in her when this was over. When the smoke cleared.

That was, if the smoke didn't choke her first.

"It's not even real," Alicia had blurted out one night, after a quarter hour of listening to Rosie rhapsodize about what a wedding to a man like Nikolai Korovin might entail, all while sitting on the couch surrounded by her favorite romance novels and the remains of a box of chocolates.

"What do you mean?"

"I mean, it's not real, Rosie. It's for show."

Alicia had regretted that she'd said anything the instant she'd said it. There'd been an odd, twisting thing inside of her that wanted to keep the sordid facts to herself. That hadn't wanted anyone else to know that when it came down to it, Nikolai Korovin needed an ulterior motive and a list of requirements to consider taking her out on a fake date.

Not that she was bitter.

"You're so cynical," Rosie had said with a sigh. "But I'll have you know I'm optimistic enough for the both of us." She'd handed Alicia a particularly well-worn romance novel, with a pointed look. "I know you sneak this off my shelf all the time. I also know that this tough, skeptical little shell of yours is an act."

"It's not an act," Alicia had retorted.

But she'd also taken the book.

If she'd stayed up too late some nights, crouched over her laptop with her door locked tight, looking through all the photos of the two of them together online, she'd never admit it. If she'd paused to marvel over the way the tabloids managed to find pictures that told outright lies—that showed Nikolai gazing down at her with something that looked like his own, rusty version of affection, for example, or showed him scowling with what looked like bristling protectiveness at a photographer who ventured too close, she'd kept that to herself, too. Because if she'd dared speak of it, she might betray herself—she might show how very much she preferred the tabloid romance she read about to what she knew to be the reality.

And then there was Nikolai.

"Kiss me," he'd ordered her a few days before they'd had to leave for Prague, in that commanding tone better suited to tense corporate negotiations than a bright little café in his posh neighborhood on a Tuesday morning. She'd frowned at him and he'd stared back at her, ruthless and severe. "It will set the scene."

He'd been different these past few days, she'd thought as she'd looked at him over their coffees. Less approachable than he'd been before, which beggared belief, given his usual level of aloofness. He'd been much tenser. Darker. The fact that she'd been capable of discerning the differences between the various gradations of his glacial cold might have worried her, if she'd had any further to fall where this man was concerned.

"What scene?" she'd asked calmly, as if the idea of kissing him hadn't made her whole body tremble with that ever-present longing, that thrill of heat and flame. "There's a wall between us and the street. No one can see us, much less photograph us."

"We live in a digital age, Alicia," he'd said icily. "There are mobile phones everywhere."

Alicia had looked very pointedly at the people at the two other tables in their hidden nook, neither of whom had been wielding a mobile. Then she'd returned her attention to her steaming latte and sipped at it, pretending not to notice that Nikolai had continued to stare at her in that brooding, almost-fierce way.

"They took pictures of us walking here," she'd pointed out when the silence stretched too thin, his gaze was burning into her like hot coals and she'd worried she might break, into too many pieces to repair. "Mission accomplished."

Because nothing screamed *contented domesticity* like an early-morning stroll to a coffee place from Nikolai's penthouse, presumably after another long and intimate night. That was the story the tabloids would run with, he'd informed her in his clipped, matter-of-fact way, and it was guaranteed to drive his ex-wife crazy. Most of Nikolai's women, it went without saying—though her coworkers lined up to say the like daily—were there to pose silently beside him at events and disappear afterward, not stroll anywhere with him as if he *liked* them.

She'd been surprised to discover she was scowling. And then again when he'd stood up abruptly, smoothing down his suit jacket despite the fact it was far too well made to require smoothing of any kind. He'd stared at her, hard, then jerked his head toward the front of the café in a clear and peremptory command before storming that way himself.

Alicia had hated herself for it, but she'd smiled sheepishly at the other patrons in the tiny alcove, who'd eyed Nikolai's little display askance, and then she'd followed him.

He stood in the biting cold outside, muttering darkly into his mobile. Alicia had walked to stand next to him, wondering if she'd lost her spine when she'd felt that giant ripping thing move through her in her flat that night, as if she'd traded it for some clarity about what had happened to her eight years ago. Because she certainly hadn't used it since. She hadn't been using it that morning, certainly. The old, spined Alicia would have let Nikolai storm off as he chose, while she'd sat and merrily finished her latte.

Or so she'd wanted to believe.

Nikolai had slid his phone into a pocket and then turned that winter gaze on her, and Alicia had done her best to show him the effortlessly polite—if tough and slightly cynical—mask she'd tried so hard to wear during what he'd called *the public phase of this arrangement*. Yet something in the way he'd stared down at her that gray morning, that grim mouth of his a flat line, had made it impossible.

"Nikolai…" But she hadn't known what she'd meant to say.

He'd reached over to take her chin in his leather-gloved hand, and she'd shivered though she wasn't cold at all.

"There are paparazzi halfway down the block," he'd muttered. "We must bait the trap, *solnyshka*."

And then he'd leaned down and pressed a very hard, very serious, shockingly swift kiss against her lips.

Bold and hot. As devastating as it was a clear and deliberate brand of his ownership. His possession.

It had blown her up. Made a mockery of any attempts she'd thought she'd been making toward politeness, because that kiss had been anything but, surging through her like lightning. Burning her into nothing but smoldering need, right there on the street in the cold.

She'd have fallen down, had he not had those hard fingers on her chin. He'd looked at her for a long moment that had felt far too intimate for a public street so early in the morning, and then he'd released her.

And she'd had the sinking feeling that he knew exactly what he'd done to her. Exactly how she felt. That this was all a part of his game. His plan.

"Let me guess what that word means," she'd said after a moment, trying to sound tough but failing, miserably. She'd been stripped down to nothing, achingly vulnerable, and she'd heard it clear as day in her voice. There'd been every reason to suppose he'd read it as easily on her face. "Is it Russian for gullible little fool, quick to leap into bed with a convenient stranger and happy to sell out her principles and her self-respect for any old photo opportunity—"

"Little sun," he'd bit out, his own gaze haunted. Tormented. He'd stared at her so hard she'd been afraid she'd bear the marks of it. She'd only been distantly aware that she trembled, that it had nothing to do with the temperature. He'd raised his hand again, brushed his fingers across her lips, and she'd had to bite back something she'd been terribly afraid was a sob. "Your smile could light up this city like a nuclear reactor. It's a weapon. And yet you throw it around as if it's nothing more dangerous than candy."

Here, now, staring out at the loveliest city she'd ever seen, as night fell and the lights blazed golden against the dark, Alicia could still feel those words as if he'd seared them into her skin.

And she knew it would be one more thing that she'd carry with her on the other side of this. One more thing only she would ever know had happened. Had been real. Had mattered, it seemed, if only for a moment.

She blinked back that prickly heat behind her eyes, and when they cleared, saw Nikolai in the entrance to her room. No more than a dark shape behind her in the window's reflection. As if he, too, was already disappearing, turning into another memory right before her eyes.

She didn't turn. She didn't dare. She didn't know what she'd do.

"We leave in an hour," he said.

Alicia didn't trust herself to speak, and so merely nodded.

And she could feel that harshly beautiful kiss against her mouth again, like all the things she couldn't allow herself to say, all the things she knew she'd never forget as long as she lived.

Nikolai hesitated in the doorway, and she held her breath, but then he simply turned and melted away, gone as silently as he'd come.

She dressed efficiently and quickly in a sleek sheath made of a shimmery green that made her feel like a mermaid. It was strapless with a V between her breasts, slicked down to her waist, then ended in a breezy swell at her knees. It had been hanging in her room when she'd arrived, next to a floor-length sweep of sequined royal blue that was clearly for the more formal ball tomorrow night. And accessories for both laid out on a nearby bureau. She slid her feet into the appropriate shoes, each one a delicate, sensual triumph. Then she picked up the cunning little evening bag, the green of the dress with blues mixed in.

He's bought and paid for you, hasn't he? she asked herself as she walked down the long hall toward the suite's main room, trying to summon her temper. Her sense of outrage. Any of that motivating almost-hate she'd tried to feel for him back in the beginning. *There are words to describe arrangements like this, aren't there? Especially if you're foolish enough to sleep with him....*

But she knew that the sad truth was that she was going to do this, whether she managed to work herself into a state or not. She was going to wear the fine clothes he'd bought her and dance to his tune, quite literally, because she no longer had the strength to fight it. To fight him.

To fight her own traitorous heart.

And time was running out. By Monday it would be as if she'd dreamed all of this. She imagined that in two months' time or so, when she was living her normal life and was done sorting out whatever Nikolai fallout there might be, she'd feel as if she had.

A thought that should have made her happy and instead was like a huge, black hole inside of her, yawning and deep. She ignored it, because she didn't know what else to do as she walked into the lounge. Nikolai stood in front of the flat-screen television, frowning at the financial report, but turned almost before she cleared the entryway, as if he'd sensed her.

She told herself she hardly noticed anymore how beautiful he was. How gorgeously lethal in another fine suit.

Nikolai roamed toward her, his long strides eating up the luxurious carpet beneath his feet, the tall, dark, brooding perfection of him bold and elegant in the middle of so much overstated opulence. Columns wrapped in gold. Frescoed ceilings. And his gaze was as bright as the winter sky, as if he made it daylight again when he looked at her.

There was no possibility that she would survive this in anything like one piece. None at all.

You can fall to pieces next week, she told herself firmly. It would be Christmas. She'd hole up in her parents' house as planned, stuff herself with holiday treats and too much mulled wine, and pretend none of this had ever happened. That *he* hadn't happened to her.

That she hadn't done this to herself.

"Are you ready?" he asked.

"Define ready." She tried to keep her voice light. Amused. Because anything else would lead them to places she didn't want to go, because she doubted she'd come back from them intact. "Ready to attend your exciting whirl of corporate events? Certainly. Ready to be used in my capacity as weapon of choice, aimed directly at your ex-wife's face?" She even smiled then, and it felt almost like the real thing. "I find I'm as ready for *that* as I ever was."

"Then I suppose we should both be grateful that there will be no need for weaponry tonight," he said, in that way of his that insinuated itself down the length of her back, like a sliver of ice. The rest of her body heated at once, inside and out, his brand of winter like a fire in her, still. "This is only a tedious dinner. An opportunity to make the donors feel especially appreciated before we ask them for more money tomorrow."

When he drew close, he reached over to a nearby incidental table and picked up a long, flat box. He held it out to her without a word, his expression serious. She stared at it until he grew impatient, and then he simply cracked open the box himself and pulled out a shimmering necklace. It was asymmetrical and bold, featuring unusually shaped clusters of blue and green gems set in a thick rope that nonetheless managed to appear light. Fun. As fanciful, in its way, as this golden city they stood in.

The very things this man was not.

"I would have taken you for the black diamond sort," Alicia said, her eyes on the necklace instead of him, because it was the prettiest thing she'd seen and yet she knew it would pale next to his stark beauty. "Or other very, very dark jewels. Heavy chunks of hematite. Brooding rubies the color of burgundy wine."

"That would be predictable," he said, a reproving note in his low voice, the hint of that dark humor mixed in with it, making her wish. *Want.*

He slid the necklace into place, cool against her heated skin, his fingers like naked flame. She couldn't help the sigh that escaped her lips, and her eyes flew to his, finally, to find him watching her with that lazy, knowing intensity in his gaze that had been her undoing from the start.

He reached around to the nape of her neck, taking his time fastening the necklace, letting his fingertips dance and tease her skin beneath the cloud of her curls, then smoothing over her collarbone. He adjusted it on her neck, making sure it fell as he wanted it, one end stretched down toward the upper swell of one breast.

Alicia didn't know if he was teasing her or tearing her apart. She could no longer tell the difference.

When he caught her gaze again, neither one of them was breathing normally, and the room around them felt hot and close.

"Come," he said, and she could hear it in his voice. That fire. That need. That tornado that spiraled between them, more and more out of control the longer this went on, and more likely to wreck them both with every second.

And it would, she thought. *Soon.*

Just as he'd warned her.

CHAPTER EIGHT

A GOLD-MIRRORED LIFT delivered them with hushed and elegant efficiency into the brightly lit foyer of the presidential suite in one of Prague's finest hotels, filled with the kind of people who were not required to announce their wealth and consequence because everything they did, said and wore did it for them. Emphatically.

These were Nikolai's people. Alicia kept her polite smile at the ready as Nikolai steered her through the crowd. This was his world, no matter how he looked at her when they were in private. No matter what stories she'd told herself, she was no more than a tourist, due to turn straight back into a pumpkin the moment the weekend was over. And then stay that way, this strange interlude nothing more than a gilt-edged memory.

She could almost feel the heavy stalk beginning to form, like a brand-new knot in her stomach.

Nikolai pulled her aside after they'd made a slow

circuit through the monied clusters of guests, into a small seating area near the farthest windows. Outside, in the dark, she could see the magnificence of Prague Castle, thrusting bright and proud against the night. And inside, Nikolai looked down at her, unsmiling, in that way of his that made everything inside of her squeeze tight, then melt.

"I told you this would be remarkably boring, did I not?"

"Perhaps for you," she replied, smiling. "I keep wondering if the American cattle baron is going to break into song at the piano, and if so, if that very angry-looking German banker will haul off and hit him."

His blue eyes gleamed, and she felt the warmth of it all over, even deep inside where that knot curled tight in her gut, a warning she couldn't seem to heed.

"These are not the sort of people who fight with their hands," Nikolai said, the suggestion of laughter in his gaze, on his mouth, lurking in that rough velvet voice of his. "They prefer to go to war with their checkbooks."

"That sounds a bit dry." She pressed her wineglass to her lips and sipped, but was aware of nothing but Nikolai. "Surely throwing a few punches is more exciting than writing checks?"

"Not at all." His lips tugged in one corner. "A fistfight can only be so satisfying. Bruises heal. Fight with money, and whole companies can be leveled, thousands of lives ruined, entire fortunes destroyed in the course of an afternoon." That smile deepened, became slightly mocking. "This also requires a much longer recovery period than a couple of bruises."

Alicia searched his face, wondering if she was seeing what she wanted to see—or if there really was a softening there, a kind of warmth, that made that wide rip in her feel like a vast canyon and her heart beat hard like a drum.

He reached over and traced one of the clever shapes that made up the necklace he'd given her, almost lazily, but Alicia felt the burn of it as if he was touching her directly. His gaze found hers, and she knew they both wished he was.

It swelled between them, bright and hot and more complicated now, that electric connection that had shocked her in that club. It was so much deeper tonight. It poured into every part of her, changing her as it went, making her realize she didn't care what the consequences were any longer. They'd be worth it. Anything would be worth it if it meant she could touch him again.

She couldn't find the words to tell him that, so she smiled instead, letting it all flow out of her. Like a weapon, he'd said. Like candy.

Like love.

Nikolai jerked almost imperceptibly, as if he saw what she thought, what she felt, written all over her. As if she'd said it out loud when she hardly dared think it.

"Alicia—" he began, his tone deeper than usual, urgent and thick, and all of her confusion and wariness rolled into the place where she'd torn in two, then swelled into that ache, making it bloom, making her realize she finally knew what it was....

But then the energy in the suite all around them shifted. Dramatically. There was a moment of shocked silence, then an excited buzz of whispering.

Nikolai's gaze left hers and cut to the entryway, and then, without seeming to move at all, he froze solid. She watched him do it, saw him turn from flesh and blood to ice in a single breath.

It was the first time he'd scared her.

Alicia turned to see the crowd parting before a graceful woman in a deceptively simple black dress, flanked by two security guards. She was cool and aristocratic as she walked into the room, smiling and exchanging greetings with the people she passed. Her dark red hair was swept back into an elegant chignon, she wore no adornment besides a hint of diamonds at her ears and the sparkle of the ring on her hand, and still, she captivated the room.

And had turned Nikolai to stone.

Alicia recognized her at once, of course.

"Isn't that…?"

"My brother's wife. Yes."

Nikolai's tone was brutal. Alicia flicked a worried glance at him, then looked back to the party.

Miranda Sweet, wife of the legendary Ivan Korovin and easily identifiable to anyone with access to Rosie's unapologetic subscription to celebrity magazines, swept through the assembled collection of donors with ease. She said a word or two here, laughed there and only faltered when her gaze fell on Nikolai. But she recovered almost instantly, squaring her shoulders and waving off her security detail, and made her way toward him.

She stopped when she was a few feet away. Keeping a safe distance, Alicia thought, her eyes narrowing. Miranda Sweet was prettier in person, and taller, and the way she looked at Nikolai was painful.

While Nikolai might as well have been a glacier.

Alicia could have choked on the thick, black tension that rose between the two of them, so harsh it made her ears ring. So intense she glanced around to see if anyone else had noticed, but Miranda's security guards had blocked them off from prying eyes.

When she looked back, Nikolai and his brother's wife were still locked in their silent battle. Alicia moved closer to Nikolai's side, battling the urge to step in front of him and protect him from this threat, however unlikely the source.

Then, very deliberately, Nikolai dropped his gaze. Alicia followed it to the small swell of Miranda's belly, almost entirely concealed by her dress. Alicia never would have seen it. She doubted anyone was supposed to see it.

When Nikolai raised his gaze to his sister-in-law's again, his eyes were raw and cold. Alicia saw Miranda swallow. Hard. Nervously, even.

Another terrible moment passed.

Then Miranda inclined her head slightly. "Nikolai."

"Miranda," he replied, in the same tone, so crisp and hard and civil it hurt.

Miranda glanced at Alicia, then back at Nikolai, and something moved across her face.

Fear, Alicia thought, confused. *She's* afraid *of him*.

Miranda hid it almost immediately, though her hand moved to brush against her belly, her ring catching the light. She dropped her hand when she saw Nikolai glance at it.

"He misses you," she said after a moment, obvious conflict and a deep sadness Alicia didn't understand in her voice. "You broke his heart."

"Are you his emissary?"

"Hardly." Miranda looked at Nikolai as if she expected a reply, but he was nothing but ice. "He would never admit that. He'd hate that I said anything."

"Then why did you?" Cold and hard, and Alicia

thought it must hurt him to sound like that. To be that terribly frigid.

Miranda nodded again, a sharp jerk of her head. Her gaze moved to Alicia for a moment, as if she wanted to say something, but thought better of it. And then she turned and walked away without another word, her smile in place as if it had never left her.

While Alicia stood next to Nikolai and hurt for him, hard and deep, and all the things he didn't—couldn't—say.

"I take it you weren't expecting her," she said after a while, still watching Miranda Sweet work the party, marveling at how carefree she looked when she'd left a wind chill and subzero temperatures in her wake.

"I should have." Nikolai's gaze was trained on the crowd, dark and stormy. "She often makes appearances at high-level donor events when Ivan is held up somewhere else. It helps bring that little bit of Hollywood sparkle."

He sounded as if he was reporting on something he'd read a long time ago, distant and emotionless, but Alicia knew better. She felt the waves of that bitter chill coming off him, like arctic winds.

This was Nikolai in pain. She could feel it inside her own chest, like a vise.

"A bit of a chilly reunion, I couldn't help but notice."

Nikolai shifted. "She believes I tried to ruin her relationship with Ivan."

Alicia frowned up at him. "Why would she think that?"

It took Nikolai a breath to look down, to meet her eyes. When he did, his gaze was the coldest she'd ever seen it, and her heart lurched in her chest.

"Because I did."

She blinked, but didn't otherwise move. "Why?"

A great black shadow fell over him then, leaving him hollow at the eyes and that hard mouth of his too grim. *Grief,* she thought. And something very much like shame, only sharper. Colder.

"Why do I do anything?" he asked softly. Terribly. "Because happiness looks like the enemy to me. When I see it I try to kill it."

Alicia only stared at him, stricken. Nikolai's mouth tugged in one corner, a self-deprecating almost smile that this time was nothing but dark and painful. Total devastation in that one small curve.

"You should be afraid of me, Alicia," he said, and the bleak finality in his voice broke her in two. "I keep warning you."

He turned back to the crowd.

And Alicia followed an instinct she didn't fully understand, that had something to do with that deep ache, that wide-open canyon in her chest she didn't think would ever go away, and the proud, still way he stood next to her, ruthlessly rigid and straight, as if bracing himself for another blow.

Like that brave boy he must have been a lifetime ago, who was never safe. Or lucky. Who had given up all hope.

She couldn't bear it.

Alicia reached over and slid her hand into his, as if it belonged there. As if they fitted together like a puzzle, and she was clicking the last piece into place.

She felt him flinch, but then, slowly—almost cautiously—his long fingers closed over hers.

And then she held on to him with all of her might.

Nikolai hadn't expected Alicia to be quite so good at this, to fill her role so seamlessly tonight, as if she'd been born to play the part of his hostess. As if she belonged right there at his side, the limb he hadn't realized he'd been missing all along, instead of merely the tool he'd planned to use and then discard.

He stood across the room, watching from a distance as she charmed the two men she'd thought might break into a fight earlier. She was like a brilliant sunbeam in the middle of this dark and cold winter's night, outshining his wealthiest donors in all their finery even here, in a luxurious hotel suite in a city renowned for its gleaming, golden, incomparable light.

Nikolai had never seen her equal. He never would again.

She'd held on to his hand. *To him*. Almost ferociously, as if she'd sensed how close he'd been to disappearing right where he stood and had been determined to stand as his anchor. And so she had.

Nikolai couldn't concentrate on his duties tonight the way he usually did, with that single-minded focus that was his trademark. He couldn't think too much about the fact that Ivan had a child on the way, no matter the vows they'd made as angry young men that they would never inflict the uncertain Korovin temper on more innocent children.

He couldn't think of anything but that press of Alicia's palm against his, the tangling of their fingers as if they belonged fused together like that, the surprising strength of her grip.

As if they were a united front no matter the approaching threat—Miranda, the pregnancy Ivan had failed to mention, the donors who wanted to be celebrated and catered to no matter what quiet heartbreaks might occur in their midst, even the ravaged wastes of his own frigid remains of a soul.

She'd held his hand as if she was ready to fight at his side however she could and that simple gesture had humbled him so profoundly that he didn't know how he'd remained upright. How he hadn't sunk to his knees and promised her anything she wanted, anything at all, if she would only do that again.

If she would choose him, support him. Defend him. Protect him.

If she would treat him like a man, not a wild animal in need of a cage. If she would keep treating him like that. Like he really could be redeemed.

As if she hadn't the smallest doubt.

Because if he wasn't the irredeemable monster he'd always believed—if both she and Ivan had been right all along—then he could choose. He could choose the press of her slender fingers against his, a shining bright light to cut through a lifetime of dark. Warmth instead of cold. Sun instead of ice. *He could choose.*

Nikolai had never imagined that was possible. He'd stopped wanting what he couldn't have. He'd stopped *wanting*.

Alicia made him believe he could be the man he might have been, if only for a moment. She made him regret, more deeply than he ever had before, that he was so empty. That he couldn't give her anything in return.

Except, a voice inside him whispered, *her freedom from this.*

From him. From this dirty little war he'd forced her to fight.

Nikolai nearly shuddered where he stood. He kept his eyes trained on Alicia, who looked over her shoulder as if she felt the weight of his stare and then smiled at him as if he really was that man.

As if she'd never seen anything else.

That swift taste of her on a gray and frigid London street had led only to cold showers and a gnawing need inside of him these past few days, much too close to pain. Nikolai didn't care anymore that he hardly recognized himself. That he was drowning in this flood she'd let loose in him. That he was almost thawed through and beyond control, the very thing he'd feared the most for the whole of his life.

He wanted Alicia more. There was only this one last weekend before everything went back to normal. Before he had his answer from Veronika. And then there was absolutely no rational reason he should ever spend another moment in her company.

He'd intended to have her here, in every way he could. To glut himself on her as if that could take the place of all her mysteries he'd failed to solve, the sweet intoxication that was Alicia that he'd never quite sobered up from. He'd intended to make this weekend count.

But she'd let him imagine that he was a better man, or could be. He'd glimpsed himself as she saw him for a brief, brilliant moment, and that changed everything.

You have to let her go, that voice told him, more forcefully. *Now, before it's too late.*

He imagined that was his conscience talking. No wonder he didn't recognize it.

Nikolai took her back to their hotel when the dinner finally ground to a halt not long after midnight. They stood outside her bedroom and he studied her lovely face, committing it to memory.

Letting her go.

"Nikolai?" Even her voice was pretty. Husky and sweet. "What's the matter?"

He kissed her softly, once, on that very hand that had held his with such surprising strength and incapacitating kindness. It wasn't what he wanted. It wasn't enough. But it would be something to take with him, like a single match against the night.

"You don't need to be here," he said quietly, quickly, because he wasn't sure he'd do it at all if he didn't do it fast. "Veronika will seek me out whether you're with me or not. I'll have the plane ready for you in the morning."

"What are you talking about?" Her voice was small. It shook. "I thought we had a very specific plan. Didn't we?"

"You're free, Alicia." He ground out the words. "Of this game, this blackmail. Of me."

"But—" She reached out to him, but he caught her hand before she could touch him, because he couldn't trust himself. Not with her. "What if I don't particularly want to be free?"

Under any other circumstances, he wouldn't have hesitated. But this was Alicia. She'd comforted him, protected him, when anyone else would have walked away.

When everyone else had.

It wasn't a small gesture to him, the way she'd held his hand like that. It was everything. He had to honor that, if nothing else.

"I know you don't," Nikolai said. He released her hand, and she curled it into a fist. Fierce and fearless until the end. That was his Alicia. "But you deserve it. You deserve better."

And then he'd left her there outside her room without another word, because a good man never would have put her in this position in the first place, blackmailed her and threatened her, forced her into this charade for his own sordid ends.

Because he knew it was the right thing to do, and for her, he'd make himself do it, no matter how little he liked it.

* * *

"But I love you," Alicia whispered, knowing he was already gone.

That he'd already melted into the shadows, disappeared down the hall, and that chances were, he wouldn't want to hear that anyway.

She stood there in that hall for a long time, outside the door to her bedroom in a mermaid dress and lovely, precarious heels he'd chosen for her, and told herself she wasn't falling apart.

She was fine.

She was in love with a man who had walked away from her, leaving her with nothing but a teasing hint of heat on the back of her hand and that awful finality in his rough, dark voice, but Alicia told herself she was absolutely, perfectly *fine.*

Eventually, she moved inside her room and dutifully shut the door. She pulled off the dress he'd chosen for her and the necklace he'd put around her neck himself, taking extra care with both of them as she put them back with the rest of the things she'd leave behind her here.

And maybe her heart along with them.

She tried not to think about that stunned, almost-shattered look in his beautiful eyes when she'd grabbed his hand. The way his strong fingers had wrapped around hers, then held her tight, as if he'd never wanted to let her go. She tried not to torture herself with the way he'd looked at her across the dinner table afterward, over the sounds of merriment and too much wine, that faint smile in the corner of his austere mouth.

But she couldn't think of anything else.

Alicia changed into the old T-shirt she wore to sleep in, washed soft and cozy over the years, and then she methodically washed her face and cleaned her teeth. She climbed into the palatial bed set high on a dais that made her feel she was perched on a stage, and then she glared fiercely at that book Rosie had given her without seeing a single well-loved sentence.

The truth was, she'd fallen in love when she'd fallen into him at that club.

It had been that sudden, that irrevocable. That deeply, utterly mad. The long, hot, darkly exciting and surprisingly emotional night that had followed had only cemented it. And when he'd let her see those glimpses of his vulnerable side, even hidden away in all that ice and bitter snow, she'd felt it like a deep tear inside of her because she hadn't wanted to accept what she already knew somewhere inside.

Alicia let out a sigh and tossed the paperback aside, sinking back against the soft feather pillows and scowling at the billowing canopy far above her.

She wasn't the too-drunk girl she'd been at twenty-one any longer—and in fact, she'd never been the shameful creature she'd thought she was. Had she tripped and fallen into any other man on that dance floor that night, she would have offered him her embarrassed apologies and then gone straight home to sort out her laundry and carry on living her quiet little life.

But it had been Nikolai.

The fact was, she'd kicked and screamed and moaned about the way he'd forced her into this—but he hadn't. She could have complained. Daniel was a CEO with grand plans for the charity, but he wasn't an ogre. He wouldn't have simply let her go without a discussion; he might not have let her go at all. And when it came down to it, she hadn't even fought too hard against this mad little plan of Nikolai's, had she?

On some level, she'd wanted all of those tabloid pictures with their suggestive captions, because her fascination with him outweighed her shame. And more, because they proved it was real. That the night no one knew about, that she'd tried so hard to make disappear, had really, truly happened.

She'd tasted him in that shiny black SUV, and she'd loved every moment of his bold possession. She'd explored every inch of his beautiful body in that wide bed of his. She'd kissed his scars and even the monster he wore on his chest like a warning. And he'd made her sob and moan and surge against him as if she'd never get enough of him, and then they'd collapsed against each other to sleep in a great tangle, as if they weren't two separate people at all.

All of that had happened. All of it was real.

All of this is real, she thought.

Alicia picked up the paperback romance again, flipping through the well-worn pages to her favorite scene, which she'd read so many times before she was sure she could quote it. She scanned it again now.

Love can't hinge on an outcome. If it does, it

isn't love at all, the heroine said directly to the man she loved when all was lost. When he had already given up, and she loved him too much to let him. When she was willing to fight for him in the only way she could, even if that meant she had to fight every last demon in his head herself. *Love is risk and hope and a terrible vulnerability. And it's worth it. I promise.*

"You either love him or you don't, Alicia," she told herself then, a hushed whisper in her quiet room.

And she did.

Then she took a deep breath to gather her courage, swung out of the high bed and went to prove it.

Nikolai sat by the fire in the crimson master bedroom that dominated the far corner of the hotel suite, staring at the flames as they crackled and danced along the grate.

He wished this wasn't the longest night of the year, with all of that extra darkness to lead him into temptation, like one more cosmic joke at his expense. He wished he could take some kind of pride in the uncharacteristic decision he'd made instead of sitting here like he needed to act as his own guard, as if a single moment of inattention would have him clawing at her door like an animal.

He wished most of all that this terrible thaw inside of him wasn't an open invitation for his demons to crawl out and fill every extra, elongated hour with their same old familiar poison.

He shifted in the plush velvet armchair and let the heat of the fire play over his skin, wishing it could warm him inside, where too many dark things lurked tonight, with their sharp teeth and too many scenes from his past.

He hated Prague, happy little jewel of a city that it was, filled to the top of every last spire with all the joyful promises of a better life even the Iron Curtain had failed to stamp out. Anywhere east of Zurich he began to feel the bitter chill of Mother Russia breathing down his neck, her snow-covered nails digging into his back as if she might drag him back home at any moment.

It was far too easy to imagine himself there, struggling to make it through another vicious winter with no end, dreamless and broken and half-mad. Feral to the bone. In his uncle's bleak home in Nizhny Novgorod. In corrupt, polluted, snow-bound Moscow with the equally corrupt and polluted Veronika, when he'd been in the military and had thought, for a time, it might save him from himself.

Or, even sadder in retrospect, that Veronika might.

Being in Prague was too much like being back there. Nikolai was too close to the raw and out-of-control creature he'd been then, careening between the intense extremes that were all he'd ever known. Either losing himself in violence or numbing himself however he could. One or the other, since the age of five.

He could feel that old version of him right beneath his skin, making him restless. On edge.

Then again, perhaps it wasn't Prague at all. Perhaps it was the woman on the other side of this hotel suite even now, with her dark eyes that saw more of him than anyone else ever had and that carnal distraction of a mouth.

He was in trouble. He knew it.

This was the kind of night that called for a bottle of something deliberately incapacitating, but he couldn't allow himself the escape. He couldn't numb this away. He couldn't slam it into oblivion. He had to sit in it and wait for morning.

Nikolai scowled at the fire while his demons danced on, bold and sickening and much too close, tugging him back into his dirty past as if he'd never left it behind.

As if he never would.

A scant second before Alicia appeared in his door, he sensed her approach, his gaze snapping to meet hers as she paused on the threshold.

He almost thought she was another one of his demons, but even as it crossed his mind, he knew better. Alicia was too alive, that light of hers beaming into his room as if she'd switched on the lamps, sending all of those things that tortured him in the dark diving for the shadows.

She'd changed out of her formal attire and was standing there in nothing but an oversized wide-necked T-shirt—a pink color, of course—that slid down her arm to bare her shoulder and the upper slope of one breast. Her curls stood around her head in abandon, and her feet were bare.

Nikolai's throat went dry. The rest of him went hard.

"It's below zero tonight," he barked at her, rude

and belligerent. *Desperate*. "You shouldn't be walking around like that unless you've decided to court your own death, in which case, I can tell you that there are far quicker ways to go."

The last time he'd used a tone like that on a woman, she'd turned and run from him, sobbing. But this was Alicia. His strong, fearless Alicia, and she only laughed that laugh of hers that made him want to believe in magic.

When he looked at her, he thought he might.

"I've come to your room wearing almost nothing and your first reaction is to talk about the weather and death," she said in that dry way of hers, and God help him, this woman was worse than all his demons put together. More powerful by far. "Very romantic, indeed. My heart is aglow."

Nikolai stood up then, as if that would ward her off. He didn't know which was worse. That she was standing there with so much of her lush brown skin on display, her lithe and supple legs, that shoulder, even the hint of her thighs—naked and smooth and far too tempting. Or that teasing tone she used, so dry and amused, that set off brushfires inside him.

His body felt as if it was someone else's, unwieldy and strange. He wished he hadn't stripped down to no more than his exercise trousers, low on his hips, the better to while away a sleepless night at war with himself.

There was too much bare flesh in the room now. Too many possibilities. He could only deny himself so much....

He scowled at her, and she laughed again.

"Relax," she said, in that calm, easy way that simultaneously soothed and inflamed him. "*I'm* seducing *you,* Nikolai. You don't have to do anything but surrender."

"You are not seducing me," he told her, all cold command, and she ignored it completely and started toward him as if he hadn't spoken. As if he hadn't said something similar to her what seemed like a lifetime ago. "And I am certainly not surrendering."

"Not yet, no," she agreed, smiling. "But the night is young."

"Alicia." He didn't back away when she roamed even closer, not even when he could see her nipples poking against the thin material of her shirt and had to fight to keep himself from leaning down and sucking them into his mouth, right then and there. "This is the first time in my life I've ever done the right thing deliberately. Some respect, I beg you."

Her smile changed, making his chest feel tight though he didn't know what it meant.

"Tell me what the right thing is," she said softly, not teasing him any longer, and she was within arm's reach now. Warm and soft. *Right there.* "Because I think you and I are using different definitions."

"It's leaving you alone," he said, feeling the stirrings of a kind of panic he thought he'd excised from himself when he was still a child. "The way I should have done from the start."

She eased closer, her scent teasing his nose, cocoa butter and a hint of sugar, sweet and rich and *Alicia.* He was so hard it bordered on agony, and the way she looked up at him made his heart begin to hit at him, erratic and intense, like it wanted to knock him down. Like it wouldn't take much to succeed.

"You vowed you didn't want to sleep with me again," he reminded her, almost savagely. "Repeatedly."

"I'm a woman possessed," she told him, her voice husky and low, washing over him and into him. "Infatuated, even."

He remembered when he'd said those same words to her in that far-off stairwell, when her scent had had much the same effect on him. Her dark eyes had been so wide and anxious, and yet all of that heat had been there behind it, electric and captivating. Impossible to ignore. Just as she was.

Tonight, there was only heat, so much of it he burned at the sight. And he wanted her so badly he was afraid he shook with it. So badly he cared less and less with every passing second if he did.

"I've never had the slightest inclination to behave the way a good man might," he began, throwing the words at her.

"That simply isn't true."

"Of course it is. I keep telling you, I—"

"You've dedicated your life to doing good, Nikolai," she said, cutting him off, her voice firm. "You run a foundation that funds a tremendous amount of charity work. Specifically, children's charities."

"I'm certain bands of activists would occupy me

personally if they could pin me down to a single residence or office." He glared at her, his voice so derisive it almost hurt, but he knew he wasn't talking to her so much as the demons in all the corners of the room, dancing there in his peripheral vision. "I take money from the rich and make it into more money. I am the problem."

"Like Robin Hood, then? Who was, as everyone knows, a great villain. Evil to the very core."

"If Robin Hood were a soulless venture capitalist, perhaps," Nikolai retorted, but there was that brilliant heat inside of him, that terrible thaw, and he was on the verge of something he didn't want to face. He wasn't sure he could.

Alicia shook her head, frowning at him as if he was hurting her. He didn't understand that— this was him *not* hurting her. This was him *trying*. Why was he not surprised that he couldn't do that right, either?

"You help people," she said in that same firm, deliberate way, her gaze holding his. "The things you do and the choices you make *help people*. Nikolai, you do the right thing *every single day*."

He didn't know what that iron band was that

crushed his chest, holding him tight, making everything seem to contract around him.

"You say that," he growled at her, or possibly it was even a howl, torn from that heart he'd abandoned years ago, "but there is blood on my hands, Alicia. More blood than you can possibly imagine."

She stepped even closer, then picked up his much larger hands in hers. He felt a kind of rumbling, a far-off quake, and even though he knew there was nothing but disaster heading toward him, even though he suspected it would destroy him and her and possibly the whole of the city they stood in, the world, the stars above, he let her.

And he watched, fascinated beyond measure and something like terrified, that tight, hard circle around him pulling tighter and tighter, as she turned each hand over, one by one, and pressed a kiss into the center of each.

The way she'd done for the creature on his chest, that she'd called *pretty*.

She looked up at him again, and her dark eyes were different. Warm in a way he'd never seen before. Sweet and something like admiring. Filled with that light that made him feel simultaneously scraped hollow and carved new.

Shining as if whatever she saw was beautiful.

"I don't see any blood," she said, distinct and direct, her gaze fast to his. "I only see you. I've never seen anything but you."

And everything simply...ended.

Nikolai shattered. He broke. All of that ice, every last glacier, swept away in the flood, the heat, the roaring inferno stretching high into the night, until he was nothing but raw and wild and *that look* she gave him took up the world.

And replaced it with fire. Fire and heat and all of the things he'd locked away for all those bleak and terrible reasons. Color and light, flesh and blood. Rage and need and all of that hunger, all of that pain, all of that sorrow and grief, loss and tragedy. His parents, taken so young. His brother, who should never have had to fight so hard. The uncle who should have cared for them. The army that had broken him down and then built him into his own worst nightmare. Veronika's lies and Stefan's sweet, infant body cradled in his arms, like hope. Every emotion he'd vowed he didn't have, roaring back into him, filling him up, tearing him into something new and unrecognizable.

"You have to stop this," he said, but when it left his mouth it was near to a shout, furious and loud and she didn't even flinch. "You can't be *kind* to a man like me! You don't know what you've done!"

"Nikolai," she said, without looking away from him, without hiding from the catastrophic storm that was happening right there in front of her, without letting go of his hands for an instant or dropping her warm gaze, "I can't be anything else. That's what *you* deserve."

And he surrendered.

For the first time in his life, Nikolai Korovin stopped fighting.

CHAPTER NINE

NIKOLAI DROPPED TO his knees, right there in front of her.

For a moment he looked ravaged. Untethered and lost, and then he slid his arms around her hips, making Alicia's heart fall out of her chest, her breath deserting her in a rush. She could feel the storm all around them, pouring out of him, enveloping them both. His hard face became stark, sensual. Fierce.

It all led here. Now. To that look in his beautiful eyes that made her own fill with tears. A fledging kind of joy, pale and fragile.

Hope.

And she loved him. She thought she understood him. So when that light in his eyes turned to need, she was with him. It roared in her too, setting them both alight.

He pulled up the hem of her T-shirt with a strong, urgent hand that shook slightly, baring her to his view, making her quiver in return. And that fire that was always in her, always his, turned molten and rolled through her, making her heavy and needy and almost scared by the intensity of this. Of him. Of these things she felt, storming inside of her.

Her legs shook, and he kissed her once, high on her thigh. She could feel the curve of his lips, that rare smile, and it went through her like a lightning bolt, burning her straight down to the soles of her feet where they pressed into the thick carpet.

And then slowly, so slowly, he peeled her panties down her legs, then tossed them aside.

Alicia heard a harsh sort of panting, and realized it was her.

"Solnyshka," he said, in that marvelous voice of his, darker and harsher than ever, and it thrilled her, making her feel like the sun he thought she was, too bright and hot to bear. "I think you'd better hold on."

He wrapped one strong arm around her bottom and the back of her thighs, and then, using his shoulder to knock her leg up and out of his way, he leaned forward and pressed his mouth against her heat.

And then he licked into her.

It was white-hot ecstasy. Carnal lightning. It seared through her, almost like pain, making her shudder against him and cry out his name. She fisted her hands in his hair, his arms were tight around her to keep her from falling, and she simply went limp against his mouth.

His wicked, fascinating, demanding mouth.

She detonated. Her licked her straight over the edge, and she thought she screamed, lost in a searingly hot, shuddering place where there was nothing left but him and these things he did to her, this wild magic that was only his. *Theirs.*

"Too fast," he rumbled, from far away, but everything was dizzy, confused, and it took her a long breath, then another, to remember who she was. And where.

And then another to understand that he'd flipped them around to spread her out on the deep rug in front of the fire.

"Nikolai," she said, or thought she did, but she lost whatever half-formed thought that might have been, because he was taking up where he'd left off.

He used his mouth again, and his hands. He

stroked deep into her core, throwing her straight back into that inferno as if she'd never found release. Soon she was writhing against him, exulting in how he held her so easily, with such confident mastery, and used his tongue, his teeth, even that smile again, like sensual weapons.

Alicia arched up against him, into him. Her hands dug at the carpet below her, and his mouth was an impossible fire, driving her wild all over again, driving her higher and higher, until he sucked hard on the very center of her heat and she exploded all around him once again.

When she came back to herself this time, he was helping her up, letting her stumble against him and laughing as he pulled her T-shirt over her head, then muttering something as he took her breasts in his hands. He tested their weight, groaned out his approval, and then pulled each hard, dark nipple into his mouth.

Lighting the fire in her all over again. Making her burn.

He picked her up and carried her to the bed, following her down and stretching out beside her, sleek and powerful, tattooed and dangerous. He'd rid himself of his trousers at some point and there was nothing between them then.

Only skin and heat. Only the two of them, at last.

For a while, it was enough. They explored each other as if this was the first time, this taut delight, this delicious heat. Alicia traced the bright-colored shapes and lines that made up his monster with her tongue, pressed kisses over his heart, hearing it thunder beneath her. Nikolai stroked his big hands down the length of her back, testing each and every one of her curves as he worshipped every part of her equally.

He didn't speak. And Alicia kissed him, again and again, as if that could say it for her, the word she dared not say, but could show him. With her mouth, her hands. Her kiss, her smile.

They teased the flames, built them slowly, making up for all those lost weeks since the last time they'd touched like this. Until suddenly, it was too much. They were both out of breath and the fire had turned into something darker, more desperate. Hotter by far.

Nikolai reached for the table near his bed and then rolled a condom down his hard length, his eyes glittering on hers, and Alicia almost felt as if he was stroking her that way, so determined and sure. She could feel his touch inside of her, stoking those flames. Making her wild with smoke and heat and need.

Alicia couldn't wait, as desperate to have him inside her again as if she hadn't already found her own pleasure, twice. As if this was new.

Because it felt that way, she thought. It felt completely different from what had gone before, and she knew why. She might have fallen hard for him the night she met him, but she loved the man she knew. The man who had saved her from a prison of shame. This man, who looked at her as if she was a miracle. This man, who she believed might be one himself.

"Kiss me," she ordered him, straddling his lap, pressing herself against his delicious hardness, torturing them both.

He took her face in his hands and then her mouth with a dark, thrilling kiss, making her moan against him. He tasted like the winter night and a little bit like her, and the kick of it rocketed through her, sensations building and burning and boiling her down until she was nothing but his.

His.

The world was his powerful body, his masterful kiss, his strong arms around her that anchored her to him. And she loved him. She loved him with every kiss, every taste. She couldn't get close enough. She knew she never would.

He lifted her higher, up on her knees so she knelt astride him, then held her there. He took her nipple into his mouth again, the sharp pull of it like an electric charge directly into her sex, while his wicked fingers played with the other. Alicia shuddered uncontrollably in his arms, but he held her still, taking his time.

And all the while the hardest part of him was just beneath her, just out of reach.

"Please…" she whispered frantically. "Nikolai, *please*…"

"Unlike you," he said in a voice she hardly recognized, it was so thick with desire, with need, with this mighty storm that had taken hold of them both, "I occasionally obey."

He shifted then, taking her hips in his hands, and then he thrust up into her in a single deep stroke, possessive and sure.

At last.

And for a moment, they simply stared at each

other. Marveling in that slick, sweet, perfect fit. Nikolai smiled, and she'd never seen his blue eyes so clear. So warm.

Alicia moved her hips, and his breath hissed out into a curse. And then she simply pleased them both.

She moved on him sinuously, sweetly. She bent forward to taste the strong line of his neck, salt and fire. She made love to him with every part of her, worshipping him with everything she had. She couldn't say the words, not to a man like Nikolai, not yet, but she could show him.

And she did.

Until they were both shuddering and desperate.

Until he'd stopped speaking English.

Until he rolled her over and drove into her with all of his dark intensity, all of that battle-charged skill and precision. She exulted beneath him, meeting every thrust, filled with that ache, that wide-open rift he'd torn into her, that only this—only he—could ever soothe.

And when he sent her spinning off into that wild magic for the third time, he came with her, holding her as if he loved her too, that miraculous smile all over his beautiful face.

At last, she thought.

* * *

"You're in love with him, aren't you?"

Alicia had been so lost in her own head, in Niko-lai, that she hadn't heard the door to the women's lounge open. It took her a moment to realize that the woman standing next to her at the long coun-ter was speaking to her.

And another moment for what she'd said to pen-etrate.

Veronika.

The moment stretched out, silent and tense.

Alicia could hear the sounds of the ball, muffled through the lounge's walls. The music from the band and the dull roar of all those well-dressed, elegant people, dancing and eating and making merry in their polite way. She'd almost forgotten that *this* was the reason she was here at all. This woman watching her with that calculating gleam in her eyes, as if she knew things about Alicia that Alicia did not.

There was nothing hard or evil-looking about Veronika, as Alicia had half expected from what little Nikolai had said of her. Her hair cascaded down her back in a tumble of platinum waves. She wore a copper gown that made her slender figure look lithe and supple. Aside from the way she looked at Alicia, she was the picture of a certain kind of smooth, curated, very nearly ageless beauty. The kind that, amongst other things, cost a tremendous amount to maintain and was therefore an advertising campaign in itself.

Alicia told herself there was no need for anxiety. She was wearing that bold, gorgeous blue dress, alive with sequins, that had been waiting for her in her room. It clung to her from the top of one shoulder to the floor, highlighting all of her curves, sparkling with every breath, and until this moment she'd felt beautiful in it. Nikolai had smiled that sexy wolf's smile when he saw her in it, and they'd been late coming here tonight. Very late.

Standing with him in this castle-turned-hotel, dressed for a ball in a gorgeous gown with the man she loved, she'd felt as if she might be the princess in their odd little fairy tale after all.

She'd let herself forget.

"Tell me that you're not so foolish," Veronika said then, breaking the uncomfortable silence. She sounded almost...sympathetic? It put Alicia's teeth on edge. "Tell me you're smart enough to see his little games for what they are."

It was amazing how closely this woman's voice resembled the ones in her head, Alicia thought then. It was almost funny, though she was terribly afraid that if she tried to laugh, she'd sob instead. She was still too raw from last night's intensity. A bit too fragile from a day spent in the aftermath of such a great storm.

She wasn't ready for this—whatever this was.

"If you want to speak to Nikolai," she said when she was certain her tone would be perfectly even, almost blandly polite, "he's in the ballroom. Would you like me to show you?"

"You must have asked yourself why he chose you," Veronika said conversationally, as if this was a chat between friends. She leaned closer to the mirror to inspect her lipstick, then turned to face Alicia. "Look at you. So wholesome. So *real*. A charity worker, of all things. Not his usual type, are you?"

She didn't actually *tell* Alicia to compare the two of them. She didn't have to, as Alicia was well aware that all of Nikolai's previous women had been some version of the one who stood in front of her now. Slender like whippets, ruthlessly so. Immaculately and almost uniformly manicured in precisely the same way, from their perfect hair to their tiny bodies and their extremely expensive clothes. The kind of women rich men always had on their arms, like interchangeable trophies, which was precisely how Nikolai treated them.

Hadn't Alicia told him no one would believe he was interested in her after that kind of parade?

"I can't say I have the slightest idea what his 'type' is," she lied to Veronika. "I've never paid it as much attention as you've seemed to do."

Veronika sighed, as if Alicia made her sad. "He's using you to tell a very specific story in the tabloids. You must know this."

Alicia told herself she didn't feel a chill trickle down her spine, that something raw didn't bloom deep within at that neat little synopsis of the past few weeks of her life. She told herself that while Veronika was partly right, she couldn't know about the rest of it. She couldn't have any idea about the things that truly mattered. The things that were only theirs.

"Or," she said, trying desperately not to sound defensive, not to give any of herself away, "Nikolai is a famous man, and the tabloids take pictures of him wherever he goes. No great conspiracy, no 'story.' I'm sorry to disappoint you."

But she was lying, of course, and Veronika shook her head.

"Who do you think was the mastermind behind Ivan Korovin's numerous career changes—from fighter to Hollywood leading man to philanthropist?" she asked, a razor's edge beneath her seemingly casual tone, the trace of Russian in her voice not nearly as appealing as Nikolai's. "What about Nikolai himself? A soldier, then a security specialist, now a CEO—how do you think he manages to sell these new versions of himself, one after the next?"

"I don't see—"

"Nikolai is a very talented manipulator," Veronika said, with that sympathetic note in her voice that grated more each time Alicia heard it. "He can make you believe anything he wants you to believe." Her gaze moved over Alicia, and then she smiled. Sadly. "He can make you fall in love, if that's what he needs from you."

Alicia stared back at her, at this woman who *smiled* as she listed off all of Alicia's worst fears, and knew that she should have walked away from this conversation the moment it started. The moment she'd realized who Veronika was. Nothing good could come of this. She could already feel that dark hopelessness curling inside of her, ready to suck her in....

But her pride wouldn't let her leave without putting up some kind of fight—without making it clear, somehow, that Veronika hadn't got to her. Even if she had.

"You'll forgive me," she said, holding the other woman's gaze, "if I don't rush to take your advice to heart. I'm afraid the spiteful ex makes for a bit of a questionable source, don't you think?"

She was congratulating herself as she turned for the door. What mattered was that she loved Nikolai, and what she'd seen in him last night and today. What she knew to be true. Not the doubts and fears and possible outright lies this woman—

"Do you even know what this is about?"

Alicia told herself not to turn back around. Not to cede her tiny little bit of higher ground—

But her feet wouldn't listen. They stopped moving of their own accord. She stood there, her hand on the door, and ordered herself to walk through it.

Instead, like a fool, she turned around.

"I try not to involve myself in other people's relationships, past or present," she said pointedly, as

if the fact she hadn't left wasn't evidence of surrender. As if the other woman wasn't aware of it.
"As it's none of my affair."

"He didn't tell you."

Veronika was enjoying herself now, clearly.
She'd dropped the sympathy routine and was now
watching Alicia the way a cobra might, when it
was poised to strike.

Leave, Alicia ordered herself desperately. *Now.*

Because she knew that whatever Veronika was
about to say, she didn't want to hear it.

"Of course he didn't tell you." Veronika picked
up her jeweled clutch and sauntered toward Alicia. "I told you, he's very manipulative. This is
how he operates."

Alicia felt much too hot, her pulse was so frantic
it was almost distracting, and there was a weight
in her stomach that felt like concrete, pinning her
to the ground where she stood. Making it impossible to move, to run, to escape whatever blow she
could feel coming.

She could only stare at Veronika, and wait.

The other woman drew close, never taking her
intent gaze from Alicia's.

"Nikolai wants to know if my son is his,"
she said.

It was like the ground had been taken out from under her, Alicia thought. Like she'd been dropped into a deep, black hole. She almost couldn't grasp all the things that swirled in her then, each more painful than the next.

Not here, she thought, fighting to keep her reaction to herself, and failing, if that malicious gleam in Veronika's eyes was any indication. *You can't deal with this here!*

She would have given anything not to ask the next question, not to give this woman that satisfaction, but she couldn't help herself. She couldn't stop. None of this had ever been real, and she needed to accept that, once and for all. None of this had ever been—nor ever would be—hers.

No matter how badly she wished otherwise. No matter how deeply, how terribly, how irrevocably she loved him.

"Is he?" she asked, hating herself. Betraying herself. "Is your son Nikolai's?"

And Veronika smiled.

Nikolai saw Alicia from the other side of the ballroom, a flash of shimmering blue and that particular walk of hers that he would know across whole cities.

He felt it like a touch. Like she could reach him simply by entering the same room.

Mine, he thought, and that band around his chest clutched hard, but he was almost used to it now. It meant this woman and her smile were his. It meant that odd sensation, almost a dizziness, that he found he didn't mind at all when he looked at her.

It meant this strange new springtime inside of him, this odd thaw.

At some point last night, it had occurred to him that he might survive this, after all.

Nikolai had lost track of how many times they'd come together in the night, the storm in him howling itself out with each touch, each taste of her impossible sweetness. All of her light, his. To bathe in as he pleased.

And in the morning, she'd still been there. He couldn't remember the last time any woman had slept in his bed, and he remembered too well that the first time, Alicia had sneaked away with the dawn.

Daylight was a different animal. Hushed, he

thought. Something like sacred. He'd washed every inch of her delectable body in the steamy shower, learning her with his eyes as well as his greedy hands. Then he'd slowly lost his mind when she'd knelt before him on the thick rug outside the glass enclosure, taking him into her mouth until he'd groaned out his pleasure to the fogged-up mirrors.

He didn't think he'd ever get enough of her.

She curled her feet beneath her when she sat on the sofa beside him. Her favorite television program was so embarrassing, she'd claimed, that she refused to name it. She was addicted to cinnamon and licked up every last bit of it from the pastries they'd had at breakfast, surreptitiously wetting her fingertip and pressing it against the crumbs until they were gone. She read a great many books, preferred tea first thing in the morning but coffee later, and could talk, at length, about architecture and why she thought that if she had it to do over again, she might study it at university.

And that was only today. One day of learning her, and he'd barely scratched the surface. Nikolai thought that maybe, this time, he wouldn't have to settle for what he could get. This time, he might let himself want...everything. Especially the things he'd thought for so long he couldn't have, that she handed him so sweetly, so unreservedly, as if they were already his.

Mine, he thought again, in a kind of astonishment that it might be true. That it was even possible. *She's mine.*

Alicia disappeared in the jostling crowd, and when she reappeared she'd almost reached him. Nikolai frowned. She was holding herself strangely, and there was a certain fullness in her eyes, as if she were about—

But then he saw the woman who walked behind her, that vicious little smile on her cold lips and victory in her gaze, and his blood ran cold.

Like ice in his veins and this time, it hurt. It burned as he froze.

"Privyet, Nikolai," Veronika purred triumphantly when the two of them finally reached him. As sure of herself as she'd ever been. And as callous. "Look who I discovered. Such a coincidence, no?"

This, he thought, was why he had no business anywhere near a bright creature like Alicia. He'd destroy her without even meaning to do it. He'd already started.

This is who you are, he reminded himself bitterly, and it was worse because he'd let himself believe otherwise. He'd fallen for the lie that he could ever be anything but the monster he was. It only took a glance at Veronika, that emblem of the bad choices he'd made and with whom, to make him see that painful truth.

"Alicia. Look at me."

And when she did, when she finally raised her gaze to his, he understood. It went off inside him like a grenade, shredding him into strips, and that was only the tiniest fraction of the pain, the torment, he saw in Alicia's lovely brown eyes.

Dulled with the pain of whatever Veronika had said to her.

He'd done this. He'd put her in harm's way. He was responsible.

Nikolai had been tested last night. He'd had the opportunity to do the right thing, to imagine himself a good man and then act like one, and he'd failed. Utterly.

All of his demons were right.

Nikolai moved swiftly then, a cold clarity

sweeping through him like a wind. He ordered Veronika to make herself scarce, told her he'd come find her later and that she'd better have the answer he wanted, and he did it in Russian so Alicia wouldn't hear the particularly descriptive words he used to get his point across.

"No need," Veronika said, also in Russian, looking satisfied and cruel. He wanted to wring her neck. "I had the test done long ago. You're not the father. Do you want to know who is?" She'd smiled at Nikolai's frigid glare. "I'll have the paperwork sent to your attorney."

"Do that," Nikolai growled, and if there was a flash of pain at another small hope snuffed out, he ignored it. He'd see to it that Stefan was taken care of no matter what, and right now, he had other things to worry about.

He forgot Veronika the moment he looked away. He took Alicia's arm and he led her toward the door, amazed that she let him touch her. When they got to the great foyer, he let her go so he could pull his mobile from his tuxedo jacket and send a quick, terse text to his personal assistant.

"Whatever you're about to say, don't," he told her when she started to speak, not sure he could keep the riot of self-hatred at bay just then. She pressed her lips together and scowled fiercely at the floor, and his self-loathing turned black.

Your first response when you feel something is to attack, Ivan had said. But Nikolai had no idea how to stop. And for the first time since he was a boy, he realized that that sinking feeling in him was fear.

He slipped his mobile back in his pocket, and guided her toward the front of the hotel, not stopping until they'd reached the glass doors that led out through the colonnaded entrance into the December night. Above them, the palatial stairs soared toward the former palace's grand facade, but this entranceway was more private. And it was where his people would meet them and take her away from him. Take her somewhere—anywhere she was safe.

Finally, he let himself look at her again.

She was hugging herself, her arms bare and tight over her body. There was misery in her dark eyes, her full lips trembled, and he'd done this. He'd hurt her. Veronika had hurt *him,* and he'd been well nigh indestructible. Why had he imagined she wouldn't do her damage to something as bright and clean as Alicia, simply to prove she could? She'd probably been sharpening her talons since the first picture hit the tabloids.

This was entirely his fault.

"Your ex-wife is an interesting woman," Alicia said.

"She's malicious and cruel, and those are her better qualities," Nikolai bit out. "What did she say to you?"

"It doesn't matter what she said." There was a torn, thick sound in her voice, and she tilted back her chin as if she was trying to be brave. He hated himself. "Everyone has secrets. God knows, I kept mine for long enough."

"Alicia—"

"I know what it's like to disappoint people, Nikolai," she said fiercely. "I know what it's like to become someone the people you love won't look at anymore, whether you've earned it or not."

He almost laughed. "You can't possibly understand the kind of life I've led. I dreamed about a father who would care about me at all, even one who shunned me for imagined sins."

"Congratulations," she threw at him. "Your pain wins. But a secret is still a—"

"Secrets?" He frowned at her, but then he understood, and the sound he let out then was far too painful to be a laugh. "She told you about Stefan."

And it killed him that Alicia smiled then, for all it was a pale shadow of her usual brightness. That she gave him that kind of gift when he could see how much she hurt.

"Is that his name?"

"He's not mine," he said harshly. "That's what she told me back there. And it's not a surprise. I wanted to be sure."

"But you wanted him to be yours," Alicia said, reading him as she always did, and he felt that band around his chest pull so tight it hurt to breathe, nearly cutting him in half.

"You want to make me a better man than I am," he told her then, losing his grip on that darkness inside of him. "And I want to believe it more than you can imagine. But it's a lie."

"Nikolai—"

"The truth is, even if Stefan was my son, he'd be better off without me." It was almost as if he was angry—as if this was his temper. But he knew it was worse than that. It was that twisted, charred, leftover thing she'd coaxed out of its cave. It was what remained of his heart, and she had to *see*. She had to *know*. "I was drunk most of the five years I thought I was his father. And now I'm—" He shook his head. *"This."*

"You're what?" Her dark eyes were glassy. "Sober?"

He felt that hard and low, like a kick to the gut. He didn't know what was happening to him, what she'd done. He only knew he had to remove her from this—get her to a minimum safe distance where he could never hurt her again, not even by mistake.

"Seeing Veronika made things perfectly clear to me," he told her. "All I will ever do is drag you down until I've stolen everything. Until I've ruined you. I can promise you that." He wanted to touch her, but he wouldn't. He couldn't risk it. "I would rather be without you than subject you to this—this sick, twisted horror show."

He was too close to her, so close he could hear that quick, indrawn breath, so close he could smell that scent of hers that drove him wild, even now.

He was no better than an animal.

Alicia looked at him for a long moment. "Are you still in love with her?" she asked.

"Do I *love* her?" Nikolai echoed in disbelief. "What the hell is *love,* Alicia?"

His voice was too loud. He heard it bouncing back at him from the polished marble floors, saw Alicia straighten her back as if she needed to stand tall against it. He hated public scenes and yet he couldn't stop. He rubbed his hands over his face to keep himself from punching the hard stone wall. It would only be pain, and it would fade. And he would still be right here. He would still be him.

"Veronika made me feel numb," he said instead, not realizing the truth of it until he said it out loud. Something seemed to break open in him then, some kind of painful knotted box he'd been holding on to for much too long. "She was an anesthetic. And I thought that was better than being alone." He glared at her. "And she didn't love me either, if that's your next question. I was her way out of a dead-end life, and she took it."

"I think that however she's capable of it, she does love you," Alicia argued softly. "Or she wouldn't want so badly to hurt you."

"Yes," he said, his voice grim. "Exactly. That is the kind of love I inspire. A vile loathing that time only exacerbates. A hatred so great she needed to hunt you down and take it out on you. Such are my gifts." He prowled toward Alicia then, not even knowing what he did until she'd backed up against one of the marble columns.

But he didn't stop. He couldn't stop.

"I was told I loved my parents," he said, the words flooding from him, as dark and harsh as the place they'd lived inside him all this time. "But I can't remember them, so how would I know? And I love my brother, if that's what it's called." He looked around, but he didn't see anything but the past. And the demons who jeered at him from all of those old, familiar shadows. "Ivan feels a sense of guilt and obligation to me because he got out first, and I let him feel it because I envy him for escaping so quickly while I stayed there and rotted. And then I made it my singular goal to ruin the only happiness he'd ever known."

He'd thought he was empty before, but now he knew. This was even worse. This was unbearable, and yet he had no choice but to bear it.

"That's a great brotherly love, isn't it?"

"Nikolai," she said thickly, and she'd lost the battle with her tears. They streaked down her pretty face, each one an accusation, each one another knife in his side. "You aren't responsible for what happened to you as a child. With all the work you do, you can't truly believe otherwise. You *survived,* Nikolai. That's what matters."

And once again, he wanted to believe her. He wanted to be that man she was called to defend. He wanted to be anything other than *this.*

"I've never felt anything like these things I feel for you," he told her then, raw and harsh, so harsh it hurt him, too, and then she started to shake, and that hurt him even more. "That light of yours. The way you look at me—the way you *see* me." He reached out as if to touch her face, but dropped his hand back to his side. "I knew it that first night. I was *happy* when you walked into that conference room, and it terrified me, because do you know what I do with *happy?*"

"You do not kill it," she told him fiercely. "You try, and you fail. Happiness isn't an enemy, Nikolai. You can't beat it up. It won't fight back, and eventually, if you let it, it wins."

"I will suck you dry, tear you down, take everything until nothing remains." He moved closer, so outside himself that he was almost glad that he was so loud, that he was acting like this so she could see with her own eyes what kind of man he was. "Do I love you, Alicia? Is that what this is? This charred and twisted thing that will only bring you pain?"

"I love you," she said quietly. Clearly and distinctly, her eyes on his. Without a single quaver in her voice. Without so much as a blink. Then she shifted, moved closer. "I love you, Nikolai."

Nikolai stilled. Inside and out. And those words hung in him like stained glass, that light of hers making them glow and shine in a cascade of colors he'd never known existed before.

He thought he almost hated her for that. He told himself he'd rather not know.

He leaned in until her mouth was close enough to kiss, and his voice dropped low. Savage. "Why would you do something so appallingly self-destructive?"

"Because, you idiot," she said calmly, not backing away from him, not looking even slightly intimidated. "*I love you.* There's always a risk when you give someone your heart. They might crush it. But that's no reason not to do it."

He felt as if he was falling, though he wasn't. He only wished he was. He leaned toward her, propping his hands on either side of her head as he had once before, then lowering his forehead until he rested it against hers.

And for a moment he simply breathed her in, letting his eyes fall shut, letting her scent and her warmth surround him.

He felt her hands come up to hold on to him, digging in at his hips with that strong grip that had already undone him once before, and he felt a long shudder work through him.

"This is the part where you run for cover, Alicia," he whispered fiercely. "I told you why I couldn't lose control. Now you know."

He heard her sigh. She tipped back her head, then lifted her hands up to take his face between them. When he opened his eyes, what he saw in her gaze made him shake.

"This is where you save yourself," he ground out at her.

She smiled at him, though more tears spilled from her eyes. She held him as if she had no intention of letting him go. She looked at him as if he was precious. Even now. "And then who saves you?"

CHAPTER TEN

NIKOLAI'S HANDS SLIPPED from the marble column behind her, his arms came around her, and he held her so tightly, so closely, that Alicia wasn't sure she could breathe.

And she didn't care.

He held her like that for a long time.

A member of the hotel staff came over to quietly inquire if all was well, and she waved him away. A trio of black-suited people who could only be part of Nikolai's pack of assistants appeared, and she frowned at them until they backed off.

And outside, in the courtyard of the former palace, it began to snow.

Nikolai let out a long, shaky breath and lifted his head. He kissed her, so soft and so sweet it made her smile.

"If I had a heart, I would give it to you," he said then, very seriously. "But I don't."

She shook her head at him, and kissed him

back, losing herself in that for a long time. His eyes were haunted, and she loved him so much she didn't know if she wanted to laugh or cry or scream—it seemed too big to contain.

And he loved her, too. He'd as much as said so. He just didn't know what that meant.

So Alicia would have to show him. Step by step, smile by smile, laugh by laugh, until he got it. Starting now.

"You have a heart, Nikolai," she told him gently, smiling up at that beautifully hard face, that perfectly austere mouth, her would-be Tin Man. "It's just been broken into so many pieces, and so long ago, you never learned how to use it properly."

"You're the only one who thinks so," he said softly.

She reached out and laid her hand on his chest, never looking away from him.

"I can feel it. It's right here. I promise."

"And I suppose you happen to know how one goes about putting back together a critically underused heart, no doubt fallen into disrepair after all these years," he muttered, but his hands were moving slow and sweet up her back and then down her arms to take her hands in his.

"I have a few ideas," she agreed. "And your heart is not a junked-out car left by the side of a road somewhere, Nikolai. It's real and it's beating and you've been using it all along."

He looked over his shoulder then, as if he'd only then remembered where they were. One of his assistants appeared from around the corner as if she'd been watching all along, and he nodded at her, but didn't move. Then he looked out the glass doors, at the snow falling into the golden-lit court-yard and starting to gather on the ground.

"I hate snow," he said.

"Merry Christmas to you, too, Ebenezer Scrooge," Alicia said dryly. She slid an arm around his waist and looked outside. "It's beautiful. A fairy tale," she said, smiling at him, "just as you promised me in the beginning."

"I think you're confused." But she saw that smile of his. It started in his eyes, made them gleam. "I promised you fangs. And tears. Both of which I've delivered, in spades."

"There are no wolves in a story involving ball gowns, Nikolai. I believe that's a rule."

"Which fairy tale is this again? The ones I re-member involved very few ball gowns, and far more darkness." His mouth moved into that crooked curve she adored, but his eyes were serious when they met hers. "I don't know how to be a normal man, Alicia. Much less a good one." His smile faded. "And I certainly don't know how to be anything like good for you."

Alicia smiled at him again, wondering how she'd never known that the point of a heart was to break. Because only then could it grow. And swell big enough to hold the things she felt for Nikolai.

"Let's start with normal and work from there," she managed to say. "Come to Christmas at my parents' house. Sit down. Eat a huge Christmas dinner. Make small talk with my family." She grinned. "I think you'll do fine."

He looked at her, that fine mouth of his close again to grim.

"I don't know if I can be what you want," he said. "I don't know—"

"I want you," she said. She shook her head when he started to speak. "And all you have to do is love me. As best you can, Nikolai. For as long as you're able. And I'll promise to do the same."

It was like a vow. It hung there between them,

hushed and huge, with only the falling snow and the dark Prague night as witness.

He looked at her for a long time, and then he leaned down and kissed her the way he had on that London street. Hard and demanding, hot and sure, making her his.

"I can do that," he said, when he lifted his head, a thousand brand-new promises in his eyes, and she believed every one. "I can try."

Nikolai stood facing his brother on a deep blue July afternoon. The California sky arched above them, cloudless and clear, while out beyond them the Pacific Ocean rolled smooth and gleaming all the way to the horizon.

"Are you ready?" Ivan barked in gruff Russian. He wore his game face, the one he'd used in the ring, fierce and focused and meant to be terrifying.

Nikolai only smiled.

"Is this the intimidating trash talk portion of the afternoon?" he asked coolly. "Because I didn't sign up to be bored to death, Vanya. I thought this was a fight."

Ivan eyed him.

"You insist on writing checks you can't cash,

little brother," he said. "And sadly for you, I am the bank."

They both crouched down into position, studying each other, looking for tells—

Until a sharp wail cut through the air, and Ivan broke his stance to look back toward his Malibu house and the figures who'd walked out from the great glass doors and were heading their way.

Nikolai did a leg sweep without pausing to think about it, and had the great satisfaction of taking Ivan down to the ground.

"You must never break your concentration, brother," he drawled, patronizingly, while Ivan lay sprawled out before him. "Surely, as an undefeated world champion, you should know this."

Ivan's dark eyes promised retribution even as he jackknifed up and onto his feet.

"Enjoy that, Kolya. It will be your last and only victory."

And then he grinned and slapped Nikolai on the back, throwing an arm over his shoulders as they started toward the house and the two women who walked to meet them.

Nikolai watched Alicia, that smile of hers brighter even than a California summer and her lovely voice on the wind, that kick of laughter and cleverness audible even when he couldn't hear the words.

"You owe him an apology," she'd told him. It had been January, and they'd been tucked up in that frilly pink bedroom of hers that he found equal parts absurd and endearing. Though he did enjoy her four-poster bed. "He's your brother. Miranda is afraid of you, and she still risked telling you how hurt he was."

He'd taken her advice, stilted and uncertain.

And now, Nikolai thought as he drew close to her with his brother at his side, he was learning how to build things, not destroy them. He was learning how to trust.

The baby in Miranda's arm wailed again, and both women immediately made a cooing sort of sound that Nikolai had never heard Alicia make before his plane had landed in Los Angeles. Beside him, Ivan shook his head. And then reached over to pluck the baby from his wife's arms.

"Naturally, Ivan has the magic touch," Miranda said to Alicia with a roll of her eyes, as the crying miraculously stopped.

"How annoying," Alicia replied, her lips twitching.

Nikolai stared down at the tiny pink thing that

looked even smaller and more delicate in Ivan's big grip.

"Another generation of Korovins," he said. He caught Miranda looking at him as he spoke, and thought her smile was slightly warmer than the last time. Progress. He returned his attention to Ivan and the baby. "I don't think you thought this through, brother."

"It's terrible, I know," Ivan agreed. He leaned close and kissed his daughter's soft forehead, contentment radiating from him. "A disaster waiting to happen."

Nikolai smiled. "Only if she fights like you."

Later, after he and Ivan spent a happy few hours throwing each other around and each claiming victory, he found Alicia out on the balcony that wrapped around their suite of rooms. He walked up behind her silently, watching the breeze dance through the cloud of her black curls, admiring the short and flirty dress she wore in a bright shade of canary yellow, showing off all of those toned brown limbs he wanted wrapped around him.

Now. Always.

She gasped when he picked her up, but she was already smiling when he turned her in his arms.

As if she could read his mind—and he often believed she could—she hooked her legs around his waist and let him hold her there, both of them smiling at the immediate burst of heat. The fire that only grew higher and hotter between them.

"Move in with me," he said, and her smile widened. "Live with me."

"Here in Malibu in this stunning house?" she asked, teasing him. "I accept. I've always wanted to be a Hollywood star. Or at least adjacent to one."

"The offer is for rain and cold, London and me," he said. He shifted her higher, held her closer.

"This is a very difficult decision," she said, but her eyes were dancing. "Are you sure you don't want to come live with me and Rosie instead? She's stopped shrieking and dropping things when you walk in rooms. And she did predict that the night we met would be momentous. She's a prophet, really."

"Move in with me," he said again, and nipped at her neck, her perfect mouth. He thought of that look on his brother's face, that deep pleasure, that peace. "Marry me, someday. When it's right. Make babies with me. I want to live this life of yours, where everything is multicolored and happiness wins."

And then he said the words, because he finally knew what they meant. She'd promised him he had a heart, and she'd taught it how to beat. He could feel it now, pounding hard.

"I love you, Alicia."

She smiled at him then as if he'd given her the world, when Nikolai knew it was the other way around. She'd lit him up, set him free. She'd given him back his brother, broke him out of that cold, dark prison that had been his life. She was so bright she'd nearly blinded him, all those beautiful colors and all of them his to share, if he liked. If he let her.

"Is that a yes?" He pulled back to look at her. "It's okay if you don't—"

"Yes," she said through her smile. "Yes to everything. Always yes."

She'd loved him when he was nothing more than a monster, and she'd made him a man.

Love hardly covered it. But it was a start.

"Look at you," she whispered, her dark eyes shining. She smoothed her hands over his shoulder, plucking at the T-shirt she'd bought him and made him wear. He'd enjoyed the negotiation. "Put the man in a blue shirt and he changes his whole life."

She laughed, and as ever, it stopped the world.

"No, *solnyshka*," Nikolai murmured, his mouth against hers so he could feel that smile, taste the magic of her laughter, the miracle of the heart she'd made beat again in him, hot and alive and real. "That was you."

* * * * *